7|10

Also by Donna Freitas

THE POSSIBILITIES OF SAINTHOOD

THIS
GORGEOUS
GAME

THIS GORGEOUS GAME

DONNA FREITAS

FRANCES FOSTER BOOKS

FARRAR STRAUS GIROUX
NEW YORK

Excerpt from "For M. in October" by Thomas Merton,
from *Eighteen Poems*, copyright © 1985 by
The Trustees of the Merton Legacy Trust. Reprinted by
permission of New Directions Publishing Corp.

All other Thomas Merton quotes excerpted from *Learning to Love:
The Journals of Thomas Merton, Volume Six 1966–1967* by Thomas Merton,
edited by Christine Bochen. Copyright © 1997 by The Merton
Legacy Trust. Reprinted by permission of HarperCollins Publishers.

First four lines of Sonnet XVII from *One Hundred Love Sonnets:
Cien Sonetos de Amor* by Pablo Neruda, translated by Stephen Tapscott,
copyright © Pablo Neruda 1959 and Fundación Pablo Neruda,
copyright © 1986 by the University of Texas Press.
Reprinted by permission of the University of Texas Press.

Distributed in Canada by D&M Publishers, Inc.
Printed in April 2010 in the United States of America
by RR Donnelley & Sons Company, Harrisonburg, Virginia
Designed by Natalie Zanecchia
First edition, 2010
1   3   5   7   9   10   8   6   4   2

www.fsgteen.com

Library of Congress Cataloging-in-Publication Data
Freitas, Donna.
    This gorgeous game / Donna Freitas.— 1st ed.
        p.   cm.
    Summary: Seventeen-year-old Olivia Peters, who dreams of becoming a
writer, is thrilled to be selected to take a college fiction seminar taught by
her idol, Father Mark, but when the priest's enthusiasm for her writing
develops into something more, Olivia shifts from wonder to confusion
to despair.
    ISBN: 978-0-374-31472-9
    [1. Teacher-student relationships—Fiction.   2. Authorship—Fiction.
3. Priests—Fiction.   4. Universities and colleges—Fiction.]   I. Title.

PZ7
[Fic]—dc22

                                                    2009018309

To Jason.
Words aren't enough

I simply have no business being [in] love and playing around with a girl, however innocently . . . After all I am supposed to be a monk with a vow of chastity and though I have kept my vow—I wonder if I can keep it indefinitely and still play this gorgeous game!

—THOMAS MERTON

THIS
GORGEOUS
GAME

ON GRATITUDE

I KNOW I KNOW I KNOW I SHOULD BE GRATEFUL. I SHOULD be grateful to have his attention. To have him take such an interest in me.

I should. I *know* I should.

I *will*. No, you *are* grateful, Olivia, I tell myself as if I am my self's imaginary friend, sitting across the table, giving advice. *Start acting grateful then,* she begs.

I have a gift. I have a gift from God, he says. So rare he hasn't seen it in all his many years. I'm the real thing, he says. I'm a once in a lifetime, he says. I'm special and it's his responsibility to take me under his wing, to make sure I don't waste my talent. It would be a sin *not* to help me, he says. It would be a sin for me *not* to take his offer of help.

But I swear to God . . . no . . . scratch that . . . I'll not be swearing to God . . . I swear to Who Knows What that his latest demand, this pile of typewritten pages he hands me with a face that says, *Please, Olivia, oh please don't be difficult and just do this for me,* is staring, no, it's glaring at me from the coffee table like a monster that might eat me. I feel like if I touch it I will go up in flames or the pages might bite.

Am I making too much of this? Isn't it just a matter of grabbing hold of the stack and moving it in front of my eyes so my eyes will begin to scan those black marks on the page which will magically arrange themselves into words that my brain will recognize and understand and *voilà*, I'm finished before I know it?

Then, when he asks, because he *will* ask, I'll be able to answer truthfully, "Yes, I read it. I *did*," and he will smile and I'll be *Good Olivia* again.

I wish I'd never won that stupid prize which is what got me noticed by him . . . no . . . what got my *writing* noticed by him which is what led to the initial introduction which somehow turned into communications and invitations and coffees and attending office hours and going to High Profile Events together—his words—even before the summer started.

He means well. He does. After all, what else could he mean?

"Olivia," my mother calls from downstairs. "Time for dinner. I made your favorite. Come on, sweetie."

"Be there in a minute," I yell back to her. The thought *Saved by dinner* passes through my mind. If it's not dinner that saves me lately, it's sleep, and if it's not sleep it's, oh, I don't know, cleaning my room, scrubbing the toilet. Just about anything sounds more appealing than dealing with some God Damn demand from *him*.

There. I did it. I took the Lord's name in vain and it doesn't feel half bad.

My cell phone rings. I don't pick up. I don't even look to see who is calling. I don't need to. I already know who it is and I already know I don't want to talk. The phone stops ringing and I remember to breathe. It rings again and I want to throw it. I don't. I look away. I shove the phone down between the couch cushions to muffle it. Suffocate it. Now a *ping!* tells me I have a text.

Ping! Ping!

I start to get up but still staring at me from the coffee table is this story I've got to read. I give the stack a good glare back—two can play at that game. But as soon as my eyes hit the title page I feel regret because seeing it makes something in my stomach go queasy. Ruins my appetite.

Gratitude, gratitude, gratitude. I will myself to feel gratitude with all of my being but my being revolts. I grab the stack and slam it facedown as if I can make it all go away.

✤ I ✤

*There is in her a wonderful sweet little-girl quality
of simplicity and openness.*

—THOMAS MERTON

ON LUCK

I FEEL DISBELIEF.

That's how it starts: with a pervasive sense of *this cannot be happening* and thinking that *no one is going to believe me when I tell them* because I don't even believe it myself. The thought *Mom is going to freak when she finds out* races through me in a wave of giddiness.

There I am in seventh period AP calc and Ms. Lewis is drawing tangent lines on the board and her arm and the chalk slope *up, up, up* and there is a knock and the door opens and Sister June our principal is standing there and I see the expression on her face and I know. *I know.* I know it right then. Sister June's eyes are on me and suddenly I can't remember anything about the slope of the tangent.

"I need Olivia Peters in the office right away," Sister June says with unmistakable joy and I am already shutting my notebook and textbook and shoving them into my bag because a girl can hope—sometimes a girl can't help but hope, you know? I try not to look at any of my classmates, who are staring, especially Ashley and Jada because they know I've been waiting, counting the days until May, but as usual my two best friends get the best of me so I glance in their direction.

They take turns holding up a series of notebook pages. Like flashcards. Back and forth. Quick. Practiced. As if they already know, too.

Just remember . . . says the first, flipped up by Jada . . .

You are poised . . . says the second, courtesy of Ash . . .

and beautiful . . .

and brilliant.

Thank you, I mouth, feeling touched they've put on such a show but still trying not to allow my mind to go *there*, when Sister June inquires, "Olivia?" and Ms. Lewis wonders, "Miss Williams and Miss Ling, is there something you'd like to share with the rest of us? Hmmm?" and I follow Sister June out the door. I am too nervous to smile so instead I stare at the dark blue folds of Sister June's habit and try to squelch the feeling of hope bubbling up in me because surely it will be dashed to bits when I get to her office and she tells me something anticlimactic like—"We are so pleased you've never missed a day of school in all your years at Sacred Heart!"—which is true, or—"You passed the AP English exam and will be getting college credit!"—not that I wouldn't be happy with this information, but let's face it, it's not *that* news I want to hear.

Sister June and I walk down the hall with its long line of lockers on either side, their red paint so chipped that if I use only my peripheral vision they look like giant abstract paintings. Sister June's skirt rustles with every step, making the only sound besides the soft *pat, pat, pat* of my black ballet flats and the purposeful tread of her thick, rubber-soled nun shoes against the carpet, so worn it's impossible to tell what color it used to be when it was new.

Every few feet Sister June glances my way and I detect the trace of a smile on her pursed lips and my heart quickens until it is beating so fast I imagine it is racing the fifty-yard dash and has left my body at the starting line.

Please, God, let it be what I think it is.

Sister June stops short because we are at the office entrance and I am so startled I almost knock her over. She looks up at me and her cheeks are flushed with pride and not makeup because nuns don't wear makeup, and she clasps my hands between her soft, wrinkled ones and whispers, "Oh, Olivia, your life is about to change," and that's when I notice her eyes are shiny and that's also when I know *I know beyond a shadow of a doubt* what is waiting on the other side of the door.

Who is waiting.

Sister June grasps the knob, twisting it. With one hand on my back she guides me or maybe encourages me or even ensures that I don't run away because this is my big moment, and we enter the reception area as a united front and *just like that* it happens, the same way I've been imagining and daydreaming all these months ever since the contest was announced in October and Ms. Gonzalez, my English lit teacher, encouraged me to enter it.

There he is. In the flesh. In person.

Looking at me.

I've never been this close to him before and I am struck by the tiny lines that web from his smiling eyes, the gleam from his perfect white teeth, his thick salt-and-pepper hair, the size of his hands, so large, the hands of a strong man. Everything about him seems to glow from within and soon I am aware that I am not the only person in the room who finds this visitor striking.

The reception staff surrounds him like he is a movie star or some other kind of celebrity or maybe even God come down from heaven to ask, *Hello how is everybody doing?* He is speaking but I can't focus on the words, I am only aware that Ms. Jones who does the school attendance is nodding her head, "Yes, yes. Yes, yes, of course," as he talks, and Ms. Aronson who does class registration is murmuring, "Hmm-hmmm," softly over and over, and Ms. Gonzalez is saying, "Oh my. This is wonderful. Wonderful! *Qué bien!* I knew she had it in her!" and beaming like she has just won teacher of the year or maybe even a Pulitzer Prize. Him, well, he looks younger in person than in the photos on his book jackets and when you see him on television, and maybe this is why all the women look at him with such admiration. Or is it adoration?

The door creaks as Sister June shuts it behind us.

Everyone turns in our direction and for a moment there is silence.

"You must be Olivia," he says then. His deep voice booms. "Olivia Peters!"

I open my mouth but nothing comes out.

"I'm Mark. Mark Brendan," he says, crossing the room with all the energy and confidence you'd expect from someone like him, extending his hand to shake mine, which Sister June passes from hers to his because I am frozen—after all, you don't meet your idol every day—and then he is grasping my hand with an enthusiasm that is thrilling and finally, *finally*, the biggest smile that has ever met the lips on my face breaks through and I say, "I can't believe you are here."

And just like that, we meet.

He and I meet and everything . . . it all . . . *begins.*

"It isn't because you won honorable mention, either." He smiles, looking down at me because he is at least a head taller. And I am tall.

"Wow, *wow* . . . I just never expected . . ." I say, because I've always loved writing but I didn't really think it would amount to anything. Still, I'm not going to deny that I've always wanted this and my mother—she's a writer, too—she's always said I have it in me. But if there is such a thing as divine intervention, of God whispering to us extraordinary things, I've no doubt that God whispers to him the words that have moved critics to claim he is one of the greatest writers of our time. "So, honorable mention," I repeat after him, trying to focus. "That's not why you're here, Father?"

And he says, "Please, call me Mark."

So I respond, "Okay, Father Mark," and look up at him, hopeful.

"I did go to meet the honorable mentions in person, too," Father Mark adds because he is charming and obviously a good, kind person. "But that's not why I am here, Olivia."

The way he says my name, it sounds like music, beautiful music that I listen to at the symphony, and I wish he would keep saying "Olivia . . . Olivia . . . Olivia" with his emphasis on the *O* as in Oh-liv-ee-aah and not *a*-livia the way most people pronounce it with a short *a*, as if my name begins with an article and I am this object named "Livia," like *liver* or just *live.*

Everyone is silent, waiting. Ms. Gonzalez's eyes well with tears. Ms. Aronson's cheeks flush and her body twists back and forth, arms wrapped around her middle like a girl with a crush. Ms. Jones keeps saying, "My, my . . . my, my, my . . ." with her hands clasped against her heart. Only Sister June seems unfazed—happy, yes, but somehow unruffled. Maybe this is a skill she learned as a nun, to be unmoved by handsome men, handsome priests. I wonder why everyone else doesn't act like Sister June does.

Like I do.

Like he is a man of God.

My dad's been out of the picture for more than a decade, but my older sister, Greenie, and I have had plenty of other dads over the years, it's just that everyone calls them Fathers instead of Dads and they are married to the Catholic Church. Priests have been coming to our house since I was little for lunch, tea, Sundays after mass, making sure Mom was okay on her own taking care of us and one big now-empty-of-a-husband house. Greenie and I, we took to these stand-in dads like kids to candy.

Now another one, another Father walks into my life.

What luck.

"Congratulations on winning the first annual Emerging Writers High School Fiction Prize, Olivia." Father Mark D. Brendan makes it official, his voice like velvet, and I want to reach out and smooth my hand across those words as they ripple the air. "In addition to getting your story published," he says, pausing, drawing the moment out, letting the strength of his connections sink in, "you will receive a $10,000 scholarship to the college of your choice, and of course, a spot in my HMU summer fiction seminar."

"My sister is a junior at Holy Mary University," I say, as if this matters and because I can't think of anything else, trying to stay calm, feet firm on the floor, resisting the urge to jump up and down because I want to appear older than my seventeen years and poised, like Ashley and Jada said I am.

"It was an easy decision."

Easy, he says. An easy decision.

Sunlight streams through the only window, its rays landing in the space between us, and I see him through the specs of dust that shine like glitter in the light.

"Your writing reveals a maturity beyond your years," he says, his eyes locking on mine for an instant, and then looks at his watch. He holds up an arm sheathed in the black shirt of a priest, the white collar around his neck providing the only contrast against this dark, sacred uniform. "But we'll have to continue this conversation later. Olivia, ladies, Sister June, I must be off." One by one, he nods at each person in the room, at each of us one last time, and I want to shout, *Don't go! Stay!* but I don't. "I'll be in touch again soon, Olivia, to discuss where we go from here. It was truly a pleasure."

Before I can say another word, a thank you, or even a *see you later,* Father Mark is at the door, opening it to leave, and I become aware that our entire encounter has taken barely a couple of minutes, though for me, the time goes by like a dream in slow motion. I wonder whether he means what he says, about being in touch again soon, but this question is answered almost immediately.

Before he leaves the room, before he goes, he turns and smiles and looks at me like I am a gift from God, and for a moment I feel like maybe I am.

ON JOY

WARM AIR TICKLES THE SKIN ON MY ARMS AND LEGS AS I walk home from school and I laugh out loud because I am happy. Carefree and wound up. At a stoplight I take a moment to breathe deep, inhaling the scent of flowering trees, leaning forward off the curb and fidgeting as if these small pushes and movements can will the signal to change from red to green and the blinking sign to Walk, like magic. The words *I won* swirl through my mind so fast they might slip right out and flutter off into the sky like a butterfly before I can catch them.

There were thousands of entries.

He picked me.

Walk says the street sign and I obey.

My cell pings with texts and I know it's Ash and Jada, but I am not quite ready to confirm what they suspect. For now I want to keep the news to myself, let it sink deep into the center of my thirsty soul like water in a garden.

Ping! Ping! Ping!

Maybe only a minute passes before I can't help myself any longer and I give in, digging the cell out of my bag and texting them, Come 4 dinner 2nite, BIG News (!!!!!!!!) SWAK, and then shove the phone back under my books. I look both ways then cross the street, heading along another block of town houses anchored by riotous springtime blooms packed into tiny city flower beds. I pass Berkeley Street, Clarendon Street—with its little park for small children but *no dogs allowed*—and Dartmouth Street which marks the halfway point between home and Sacred Heart, a journey I love when the weather is nice like today, but loathe in the slushy, icy muck that accumulates during a Boston winter. The sun is bright on my side of the street so I jaywalk to the center park that runs along Commonwealth Avenue, with its canopy of leafy trees that dapple the light. Pink petals fall from the blossoms above when they are shaken by the breeze and make a scattered springtime carpet across the grass. The beauty of the park reminds me of my story.

The Girl in the Garden.

Ms. Gonzalez thought it was a winner from the very beginning. It made her cry the first time she read it. "It's heartbreaking," she said, brushing a tear from her cheek. Then she asked: "Is it about your dad leaving?"

"I don't know" was my response.

The opening line: *Arturo sat on a bench under a weeping willow, a magic umbrella with its long hanging vines like locks of hair from a beautiful girl.* It takes place by the lake in Boston's Public Garden. The story is about two people who fall in love over a series of long evenings while sitting, talking on the bench. Then the girl disappears and Arturo's heart shatters.

"What's got you all happy?" A shout pulls at me and I turn to see Ash and Jada running across Commonwealth Ave. In a matter

of seconds they are beside me in the park and the sound of traf-
fic traveling down the street on either side seems far away. As my
body and mind reawaken to the world, a grin spreads across my
face until it becomes huge. My friends smile back at me and suddenly I feel nervous to say my news out loud.

"Tell us," Jada demands.

"We couldn't wait till dinner," Ash explains.

My two friends are the only people besides Ms. Gonzalez
who read my story—read every draft and talked me through
every word, sentence, and idea I hemmed and hawed about. They
listened, too, sitting on the floor of my room, full of patience, as
I told them about Ms. Gonzalez's suggestion that my dad somehow crept into my writing without my permission, without my
awareness. Without an invitation.

"So did you get in trouble with Ms. Lewis?" I stall.

"Olivia." Ash's impatience grows.

"Well?" Jada has my arm now.

"I won," I whisper.

"First prize?" Ash's voice is hesitant. Hopeful.

"First prize," I confirm.

Suddenly the three of us are screaming and jumping up and
down and doing silly, celebratory dances until we work ourselves
into a sweat.

"As soon as Sister June showed up to get you out of class, we
totally knew. Didn't we?" Ash turns to Jada for confirmation and
Jada is nodding her head yes.

"It hasn't really hit me yet."

"Don't worry, it will. Wow." Jada's mouth forms a big O.

"He gave me the news in person."

"The author?" Ash asks.

"Yeah. It was crazy. Surreal."

"Was he nice?"

"So nice." All the feelings from earlier this afternoon come rushing back and my face flushes with the memory. "I just stood there, soaking it up and telling myself over and over, *This is really happening, this is really happening*, and wanting to pinch myself to make sure."

"I'm so happy for you," Jada says.

"Well, I'm glad because it really would be a shame to waste that brain of yours," Ash says, with a playful roll of her eyes. "Did you tell your mom yet?"

"No. I'm waiting to tell her in person. Want to come back to the house with me?"

"Yes," they say.

"Mom is going to faint." I laugh when I try to picture her expression.

"We'll watch out for falling bodies then. Let's go," Jada says, and the three of us cross the street toward my house to tell my mother the good news.

The Gospel of Olivia Peters. Ha.

Jada beats me up the front steps and flings open the front door and I go flying through the foyer and into the living room. I swoop down on my mother, who is on the couch drinking her afternoon tea and talking to Father MacKinley, our parish priest, having one of their weekly chats. Ash and Jada occupy Father with polite *hello, how are you*'s, while I wrap my arms tight around

Mom and say, "I won!" She gasps and draws me close, crying out, "Olivia, I'm so proud of you!" and by now Ash and Jada have explained things to Father and I hear them laughing, Father MacKinley exclaiming, "Oh, that's wonderful," and I think how if this was a scene in a story it would be the moment when the protagonist feels the world is made entirely and perfectly of love.

ON FATE

THE NEXT DAY ASH, JADA, AND I WALK TO HOLY MARY University after school so I can register for my summer class. We get detoured the second we arrive by all the guy potential. Even though spring semester exams are in full swing, students are everywhere, enjoying the weather. Some lie on blankets in the sun, some play Frisbee. Here and there others sit reading with their backs against the trunks of the old, gnarled apple trees dotting the edges of the quad. I am already in love with the idea of being a college student here. For a couple of months at least.

We decide to wait for my sister—Greenie's living on campus through the summer—by the steps in front of Gregory Hall, right at the edge of the quad in prime people-watching territory.

"It's okay, you know." Ash turns to me.

"What is?"

"To appreciate the hot guys checking you out," Jada says, but is unable to tear her eyes away from the soccer game to our left.

"How do you know they aren't checking *you* out?"

"Um, because they're not looking at us." Ash says this like

she's stating the obvious, but to me, nothing in the boy department is ever obvious.

"Or maybe it's the fact that we scream Sacred Heart High School." The three of us are still wearing our uniforms, plaid skirts and all, and stick out like a sore thumb.

"All I'm saying is that if you're not careful, you'll break some hearts this summer."

"I will not," I protest. "You know I'm not like that."

"Tell that to Will Porter."

"I just kissed him at a dance."

"Yes, after leading him on for six months and then—" Jada holds up her hands in a heart, her attention no longer on the soccer game, and then cracks the heart open.

"Can we please not talk about this again?" Jada gets a glare from me for the physical demonstration. "Will Porter didn't even like me which is why it didn't go anywhere."

"You are blind sometimes." Jada turns back to her boy-watching.

I cross my arms over my chest, eyes darting around, self-conscious now that people, boys, are looking at me and somehow I am simply oblivious to it.

"Good thing we go to an all-girls school," Ash says, trying to lighten up the mood again. "And don't deny the fact that your eyes are practically popping out of your head."

"Not true," I say, but Ash is right. There are cute guys everywhere I turn and it's impossible not to notice. It's as if HMU decided to hold a cute guys festival this afternoon.

"Let's get a better view," Jada says, dragging the two of us closer to the soccer game. The sun shines above the gothic, ivy-covered buildings, giving everything and everyone a summery glow. The grass feels lush through my thin-soled flats. We eventually stop under a nearby tree, shading ourselves from the sun. Jada continues speaking but I no longer catch anything.

I'm distracted by a boy.

My heart begins to pound. He's bouncing a soccer ball—knee to knee to instep to knee—diagonally to my right. It's difficult not to move closer, like he suddenly has me in his gravitational pull, and I can't help but admire his dark features, the way his T-shirt shifts against his body as he moves, so fluid, so graceful and quick to meet the ball as it ascends, descends, ascends with every bounce.

"Olivia. Hey." Ash snaps her fingers in front of my face and I start. She is grinning. "See something you like?"

"No," I warn. Ashley is famous for acting rash. "Don't get any ideas."

"*Moi?* Ideas?"

I take two big steps away from her, just in case.

"Olivia!"

I turn and see my sprite of a sister half running, half walking toward us, dragging her boyfriend, Luke, behind her. Greenie and Luke have been courting—yes, courting, as in the olden days—since January. He's also an HMU student and super Catholic like she is. When they are only a few paces away, Greenie drops Luke's hand and soon I am engulfed in a hug.

"Congratulations on your big win! I'm so happy for you." Greenie speaks into my shoulder since she is a full head shorter. "Hey, Jada. Ash." She pulls back, giving them a wave.

"Nice work, Olivia," Luke says.

"Thanks, Luke. Good to see you, as always." Luke gives me a guy-style hug—a one-arm-around-the-shoulders squeeze—and then steps away to say hi to someone he knows passing by, giving Greenie and me space to do our sisterly catching up.

"I'm not at all surprised."

"I wish people would stop saying that."

"That's because we weren't surprised, either," Ash explains to Greenie.

"You've always been the smart one in the family."

"New topic, please."

"Tell me all about Father Mark. What was he like?" Greenie wants to know.

"You haven't met him? But he teaches here."

"He's one of HMU's trophy professors. Impressive for the school to list as faculty but only on campus, like, once a year. The summer class you're taking, for example."

"He didn't strike me as the inaccessible type," I say, recalling our encounter yesterday, feeling thrilled all over again. "But to answer your question: he was really nice. I was a bit starstruck. It felt like a big deal."

"He is a big deal. I bet Mom freaked when you told her about winning. She thinks he's God's gift to the novel, just like you," Greenie adds.

"Freak she did," Jada confirms, and proceeds to relay my mother's reaction in minute detail, followed by Father MacKinley's, until my cheeks are as red as Greenie's sundress.

"So," Ash says, after the embarrassing commentary subsides. "Who is that guy over there? I think Olivia would like an introduction."

"Ashley Williams, don't you—" I start, but my protest is wasted because Greenie is gone before I can stop her, tugging on Luke's arm. He bends down so she can whisper in his ear, turns toward the soccer game, and soon he is off walking toward soccer boy. "I am going to kill you. And Greenie's next."

"No you won't. You love us too much." Ash moves away from my reach just in case. "Maybe a college boy will better be able to handle your many charms," she says, and gives me her *I'm totally innocent* face.

"Whatever, Ash."

Greenie wears a grin when she returns. "So! You like Jamie Grant."

"Don't you have exams to study for or something?" I say, and roll my eyes skyward, wishing myself out of this situation.

"Everyone here knows who he is," Greenie says, ignoring my question. "He's a perfect specimen of the male species, after all."

"Please, Greenie . . ." My voice fades when I see Luke walking our way with the boy whose name is apparently Jamie and another guy. "Doesn't anyone here study?" I wonder under my breath.

"Look who's coming over to say hello," Ash says, giddy, rubbing her hands together in anticipation of watching me fumble my way through a conversation with a hot college boy.

"Sam and Jamie," Luke says when the three of them arrive, "this is my girlfriend, Greenie, her sister, Olivia," he says and I want to hug him for not qualifying me as *little* or worse, *kid*, "and Olivia's friends Ashley and Jada."

There are handshakes all around, not to mention shaking in general on my part out of nerves, especially when Jamie catches my eyes.

"I'm Jamie," he says, extending his hand.

"Olivia Peters," I say, taking it, holding on a little too long.

"Nice to meet you," says the friend.

I try to tear myself away from Jamie but I can't. I'm fixated on the thin silver chain around his neck, a tiny cross, just visible above his faded T-shirt. I am intoxicated by his nearness, bordering on mesmerized.

"I'm Sam," the friend adds, and I have to focus on him for real. I don't want to be rude.

"Nice to meet you," I say, feeling grateful when Jada takes over, happy to steer Sam's attention away from me to her.

"So you go to Sacred Heart?" Jamie asks.

"We're going to be seniors there." Despite the fact that I'm still wearing my uniform, I want to seem as mature as any other girl walking around the HMU quad.

"Luke said you're taking a class here this summer—well, *the* class," he says, sounding impressed. "It's virtually impossible to get a spot in Father Mark's seminar, you know. You are one lucky person. Though, Luke was quick to brag that it wasn't luck, but because you won a big writing contest." His smile is brilliant and I bask and glow in its light. "Sam and I are both trying to get the endless signatures of approval we need to get into it. Sign our souls over to the devil, that sort of thing."

Did I hear him right? "You're taking Father Mark's seminar?"

"Trying to," he corrects me.

"I'm sure you'll get in," I say, thinking, *Please, let Jamie in!*

So we stand there, Jamie and I, smiling at each other. Shy. Neither of us knowing what to say next.

"On that note," Greenie comes to the rescue, grabbing my arm, pulling me toward Gregory Hall since I am in a bit of a daze. "I'm going to walk Olivia over to the registrar," she calls back over her shoulder.

Luke, Jamie, Ash, and Jada and Sam—deep in conversation now—follow behind us.

"Yes. Right," I say, coming to. "Registering for class."

"Yes, my dear. The real reason you came here today, remember?" Greenie whispers into my ear, chuckling. "Well, and to see me."

"Absolutely."

"That started off well," Greenie says, nonchalant. Much subtler than Ash. "He was all dreamy-eyes for you."

"Do you think?"

"Definitely. Though, no surprise there."

"Oh, come on, G."

"I'm not sure what I think of you going out with a college guy."

"Don't get ahead of yourself. I may never see him again."

"Doubtful. Besides, you never know, he might get into Father Mark's class . . ." Greenie glances back at everyone, still following behind us. "Looks like Jada and Sam have made, um, a connection."

"They'll be trading contact info before we leave," I say, turning to look at the two of them, eyes glued to each other, talking about what, I wish I knew. If only I had Jada's powers of boy-conversation.

We cross the wide, slate courtyard and Greenie stops in front of the door to Gregory Hall. "We'll wait outside for you. I'll keep an eye on Ash and Jada. Make sure no one wanders off." She takes in the scene Jada and Sam are making now, their heads thrown back laughing, like they've known each other forever. Then, turning back to me, she says, "Go straight down the hall, through the center of the building, and you'll see the registrar's office on the right."

"Sounds like a plan." I take one last look at Jamie—who smiles when our eyes meet—before I grab the handle to the entrance hoping it will keep me from floating away with giddiness. I pull on the heavy door and feel the air-conditioning rush outside. An old-fashioned directory is mounted on the wall to the left, the kind with the white block letters that you can arrange and rearrange along the grooves. It tells me that the "Regstrar"—it's missing the *i*—is room 132. Mosaic tiles in shades of red and cream are set into the floor and form diamond patterns with the HMU crest at their center. I move through the corridor slowly, taking in the beauty of the carved wood designs between the door frames, until I reach the middle of the building and stop for a moment to look up. A cathedral ceiling reaches four stories high, with stained-glass windows at the very top that sparkle a million colors in the sun.

It's stunning.

Maybe I'll go to college here like Greenie, I think as I move on, eventually arriving at the registrar.

"How can I help you?" The man behind the counter smiles when I walk through the door.

"I'm here to sign up for Father Mark Brendan's summer seminar," I say, as Sister June instructed this morning at school.

The man's face falls, anticipating my disappointment. "You

need special permission from the professor. I'm sorry—I won't be able to do anything without his signature, the English chair's signature, and the dean's."

"But I have special permission," I explain, feeling a burst of pride as I present the paperwork Sister June gave me.

He glances at the letter and picks up the phone. "Dr. Schaeffer. You have someone here to see you. For Father Mark's class," he adds before hanging up.

A man in a coat and tie steps out of a fancy adjoining office.

"You must be Olivia Peters," he says, approaching the counter. "I'm Dr. Schaeffer, Dean of Undergraduate Studies." He smiles and offers his hand, which I take.

"Um, yes, I'm Olivia. Hi. Nice to meet you."

"Father Mark made sure we had everything ready for our special new student." Kind eyes blink behind Dr. Schaeffer's horn-rimmed glasses. "Congratulations."

"Thank you. Wow. How nice of him."

"I've known Mark for many years—he's been trying to get this contest going for a long time and is understandably excited to have the first winner announced. It's a great honor for HMU, too." Dr. Schaeffer pushes a form across the counter and hands me a pen. "All you need to do is sign here to make it official." He points to a line marked with an X. "Here, too. Then your initials here."

With each signature I am more excited, feeling like anything and everything is possible. The world at my fingertips. After initialing the last line, I return the pen and form to Dr. Schaeffer.

"You're all set, Ms. Peters."

"Thank you."

"My pleasure. Enjoy the rest of this beautiful day and we'll see you in June."

"You will." I smile wide. There is a spring in my step as I leave the office and head back down the corridor. When I reach the part with the cathedral ceiling I can't help but pause, this time taking in the gargoyles and other mythical creatures that guard the upper reaches—when I hear my name.

"Olivia? What a surprise!"

Oh-liv-ee-aah.

Father Mark stands not two feet away. In one hand is a briefcase and clasped across his chest a manuscript, or maybe just a stack of papers. He's dressed exactly the same as yesterday—black pants, long-sleeved black shirt, white collar—but this churchlike space seems a more appropriate setting for someone like him than the cramped front office at Sacred Heart.

"Hi, Father. I just registered for the class." *The* class.

"I'll take that to mean you are looking forward to it."

"I am. Really." I beam. "By the way, yesterday I was in such shock, you know, about winning, that I don't know if I expressed how grateful I am. That you picked me. I mean, for picking my story. You know, I didn't say thank you and all that."

"No need, Olivia." Father Mark is matter-of-fact. "You deserve the honor. I didn't pick a winner out of kindness." He tilts his head, looks at me in a way I don't know how to describe. "You are quite something, aren't you?" His voice is soft, faraway, when he says this and I don't know how to respond. Then, as if suddenly remembering where he was headed, he snaps back to attention and says, all business, "I'm on my way to a meeting with the provost.

I'll be in touch again before you know it—I meant what I said yesterday. It's wonderful to run into you. Just wonderful."

Before I can smile and say, "Bye, Father," he is off, down the corridor in the other direction, so I continue on my way, feeling elated that Father Mark was nice to me for the second time. Which means yesterday wasn't a total fluke.

I feel positively shined upon by fate.

When I reach the door I push my way outside into the blinding sun and shield my eyes with one hand, looking for Greenie, Luke, my friends—I search for Jamie, too, but he is gone. So is Sam. But I feel sure that Greenie is right: I'll have other chances to see Jamie and this possibility puts a smile on my face. Ash, Jada, my sister, and Luke stand talking, waiting for me by the stairs along the edge of the quad. I hesitate a moment, out on the courtyard, not quite ready to leave. Deep inside my soul I can feel things happening, stirring, big things, *good* things. Energy and excitement pulse through me. Father Mark's comment about seeing me as a *wonderful surprise* repeats in my mind. That's when I call out to everyone, letting them know that I'm back. That I'm ready.

"Let's go," I shout, and take off in a run.

ON INVITATIONS

IN THE EARLY QUIET OF THE SCHOOL DAY I TIPTOE THROUGH the corridor on the balls of my feet. The windows to the courtyard are open wide, calling the breeze inside, and it swirls around my arms and legs. I close my eyes and take a deep breath. Stand still for I don't know how long. Ever since hearing the news about the contest, I veer between abandonment to utter joy and moments when I move as if I must not disturb anything, not even make a wrinkle in the air, as if the slightest stir might sink this buoy of goodness, this gift that seems not quite true or real.

Nearing my locker, I inhale, sharp. A white rectangle sticks to the chipped red surface, a tiny paper raft floating in a long rusty river. Forgetting the slow hesitancy my body has adopted this morning, I rush forward to see what's there, bend down to read the envelope taped just above the lock.

Olivia Peters it says, handwritten in jagged, harsh cursive.

I peel it away from the metal, noticing the tiny red flecks of paint stuck to the Scotch tape. I slide my finger under the flap. Inside is a note, the same spiky handwriting dashed in a few short lines across steel gray paper.

> *Dear Olivia,*
>
> *It was wonderful to run into you yesterday. Providential. Today, if you are free—I am guessing you are free?—I'll meet you after school at Eastern Standard, 4 p.m. We can have a drink and begin to go over the edits on your story. In case you need to reach me, my cell is 617-555-7787.*
>
> *Yours, Mark*

God knows how long I stand there, staring, rereading the note in my hands, wondering when he left it. Just moments before I arrived? My lips mouth the words—*drink, notes, yours, Mark.*

"What's up with Olivia?" Ash's voice is near, but I don't look up.

"Maybe it's a love letter?" Jada says, closer now.

Their faces appear in my line of sight, ducked down and staring. "Olivia?" Ash and Jada inquire, jolting me from my trance. Ashley's huge eyes blink at me, and Jada's long black hair falls across the paper.

"What is that?" Ash snatches my precious invitation and I let out a yelp. "Dear Olivia," she says under her breath, mumbling her way through, raising her voice only when she gets to the end, shouting, "*Yours*, Mark? What are you, best buds, after like, what, a few days?"

Jada grabs it from Ash, holding it so close to her face I worry her shiny red lipstick is going to rub off on the stationery.

"Watch it," I warn. "Don't kiss my note."

"Ooooh, Olivia's got a da-ate."

"Eww, gross." I grab at the paper, but Jada holds it high and away between the tips of her dark purple, manicured nails. My face colors at the insinuation. "He's a priest, Jada."

"Calm down. Just kidding." Jada lowers her arm and hands the note back.

"Father Mark is older than my *mom*."

"Yeah, but like every other man, he's still got eyes," Ash says, laughing.

"And you're beautiful." Jada swings her locker open so I can see my face in the mirror she's hung inside the door. "I doubt a little vow is going to affect whether he notices this particular detail about you."

"Or the fact that he's older," Ash adds.

I know they're only kidding but this doesn't stop my cheeks from flushing with embarrassment and maybe even a dash of anger.

"Hey. We're just playing around, Livvy." Ash only calls me "Livvy" when she thinks she's overstepped. "We didn't mean to offend you about something you should be, like, over the moon about." She gestures at the invitation.

"Seriously." Jada agrees. "Only good intentions. Swear. Cross our hearts. All that stuff."

"Okay," I say after a long silence.

Ash smiles, leans against her locker with something like relief. "Let's get back to the important business: you get to spend the afternoon with your literary idol!" Her enthusiasm is forced, but I appreciate the effort.

"Before you guys made things seem potentially weird"—I stop, a little hesitant to continue—"I was pretty excited."

"As you should be. It's great you get to be all writerly and dream-come-true and everything. Really." The expression in Jada's eyes is genuine.

"I think Father Mark is just being nice. He's so . . . I don't know . . ." I try to find the words to describe our encounter at HMU, conjure Father Mark's image, standing there, looking at me like he saw something there, something special or intriguing that no one else has ever noticed, that has nothing to do with my looks which is what everyone else always seems to see first and then never move beyond. "He doesn't talk down to me and he acts like he's just a normal person and not someone famous. But he's probably just paying a lot of attention to the first winner."

"Well, lucky you."

"I second Jada." A smile plays on Ash's lips. "Especially after hanging out at HMU . . ." Her voice trails off, eyes dreamy.

"I wish I was taking a summer class there," Jada says, sounding wistful.

"I'm sure," I say, knowing full well that Jada would rather be boy-watching than sweating through a seminar. "Turn around and let me braid your hair," I offer, tucking the note from Father Mark into the pocket of my bag. Jada swivels so her back is to me and I gather her long, thick hair into my hands. "Stop bouncing," I direct as I part it into threes and begin crisscrossing the locks into a loose braid down her back. "Did Sam get in touch yet?"

"No," she says with a big sigh.

"Don't worry. He will," Ash reassures.

"I agree," I say. "Besides, it's only been a couple of days."

"I thought we really connected."

"You certainly looked like you did," Ash says.

"So what's on the agenda after school today?" Jada wants to know, changing the topic.

"How quickly we forget. Dear Olivia is meeting her new

literary mentor at a bar." Ash inspects her nails, lacquered a pearly white that shines bright against her dark skin.

"It's not a bar," I protest.

"It is too a bar," Ash confirms.

"It's a restaurant. And can we not do this again? The insinuations of weirdness?"

"You misunderstand—this is just how it starts. You hang out with artsy people in artsy places like bars—"

"—and cafés," Jada continues.

"—where everyone smokes cigarettes all day, guzzling whiskey or drinking espresso from tiny cups—"

"—and pretty soon it's just Ash and me IM'ing every night. Only a distant memory from your past." Jada sighs.

"Whatever." I dismiss them and take a gray sparkly elastic from Ash to secure the end of Jada's braid. I turn her around so she is facing me, surveying my work. "It's just one meeting."

"Sure, sure. You say that now."

"*Jada.*"

"We're just kidding around," Ash assures me.

"Yeah. You know we're happy for you," Jada says, and her glossy lips stretch into a grin.

"Truer words have not been spoken."

Before I can respond, Ash puts an arm around my shoulders and Jada slides one around my waist and the two of them tug me down the hall toward our first class as the bell rings.

I smile through the day—French, American history, PE, then lunch with Jada and Ash followed by physics, calculus, and finally English lit with Ms. Gonzalez. She still can't stop talking about the contest, which makes me red and embarrassed but happy, too.

In between the chatting with Ash and Jada and the note-taking and the raising of hands and talking in class about this historical era and that scientific experiment, I reread the invitation and daydream—about this afternoon and how life can change so quickly, in a single moment and in so many ways. I decide to welcome all of it, the possibilities, the opportunities, with open arms, heart, body, soul, because why wouldn't I?

ON GIRLS IN BARS

I FEEL SHY AS I SIT, LEGS CROSSED, DANGLING, AND THINK how childish my short socks and school shoes must look, one foot twitching in a nervous rhythm. Father Mark carries the conversation.

Turns out Ash and Jada are right. It *is* a bar. It's totally a bar.

I. Am. At. A. Bar.

Father Mark is waiting when I arrive at Eastern Standard, but I don't see him. Not at first. Goose bumps freckle my arms and legs as I search the sea of dark walnut tables and chairs. Men in suits are everywhere, men who look like bankers and lawyers, men clutching squat wide glasses that clink with ice or who balance clear liquid threatening to spill over the wide rim of martini glasses, men who glance up at me and make me feel self-conscious, like a girl dressed in a high school uniform in a bar because that is what I am: a schoolgirl in a bar. A few women are scattered here and there, also in suits, presumably doing business, too, clutching cocktails like the men. This is clearly a man's establishment and I am out of place.

Just when I begin to panic, worry that we were supposed to

meet somewhere else or that he is going to stand me up, I see Father Mark sitting on one of the tall, red-leather-backed chairs at the far end of the bar, his left hand gripping one of those squat glasses with the clinking ice and coppery liquid—he later tells me it's scotch, that he always drinks scotch. A book lies open in front of him but his attention is on the bartender and they are chatting.

I breathe deep, smooth my hands across my uniform, shake my long hair out of habit, and press forward with as much confidence as I can muster.

"Here she is!" Father Mark smiles, looks away from the bartender as I approach, as if he can sense me coming, and I laugh a little, feeling timid. "How nice to see you, Olivia. I've been looking forward to starting our sessions."

Sessions plural? It's my turn to smile.

"Have a seat," he says.

I hop up on the barstool Father Mark pats next to him like an obedient puppy. I do my best to sit up straight.

"What would you like?" Father Mark wants to know, and without thinking out pops, "Do you have any hot chocolate?" because the air in this place is chilled to accommodate men in hot suits on warm spring days and not girls in short sleeves and skirts with no stockings and I am shivering.

The bartender and Father Mark laugh when they hear my order and I realize that not only do I look like a kid but I order like one, too.

"Whatever you'd like, sweetheart." The bartender chuckles, and pushes through a short door that must lead to some kind of pantry.

I guess they don't keep the makings for hot chocolate up front with the liquor.

"It's cold in here," I try to explain.

"Well, they don't set the temperature for girls dressed like you," Father Mark says and I nod my head, agreeing—it's as if he's just read my thoughts—but at the same time feeling even more self-conscious.

"What are you reading?" I lean a little toward him, trying to decipher the title along the top of the page in his open book, wanting to change the subject, wishing I'd been given a manual for this situation, something like *How to strike up conversations with people you admire.*

Before Father Mark can answer, the bartender returns with a steaming mug of what looks like chocolate powder not quite mixed with hot water. "A Swiss Miss for the young lady!"

Swiss Miss? Young lady? I might die of embarrassment. "What are you reading?" I repeat, peering closer, trying to shift attention away from my drink and the bartender, who is smirking.

"Borges. *Ficciones.*" Father Mark holds up the book, turning it around so I can see the title.

"Which story?" I ask, awed by the coincidence.

"The Library of Babel," he says, the ends of his mouth creeping upward.

"That's my favorite," I manage after an excited gasp.

"I know."

"You do?"

"Your essay," he states, simple, obvious.

"Oh. Right. The personal statement for the contest."

"Yes." Father Mark slides a red bookmark into the crease on

the page. The leather strip is stamped with gold lettering and it shines for a moment in the lamplight overhead. He shuts the book and pushes it toward me, an invitation to say or do something but I don't know what. "I need to be familiar with my subject if I am going to comment effectively on your work."

Wow, I think, feeling surprised that he would be so invested that he would take time to read books by people I read, to familiarize himself with me. I am too overcome to say anything so I smile and remain silent.

"Tell me: what do you like about Borges?"

And the quiz begins.

"Well . . . his stories are wonderful . . ." I stop, wanting to choose my words with care, hoping to erode the girlish impression I've given so far. "I love the style of the Latin American writers—you know, magic realism and all that. But I love the Americans, too. The classics, like Fitzgerald, but especially Percy and Flannery. Flannery O'Connor I mean. In our house we call her by her first name as if she's a family friend," I add as if this explains everything.

"You don't look the type." Father Mark's eyes narrow.

"What type?" I twirl a lock of hair around my fingers out of habit, or maybe out of nerves.

"Bookish. Writerly." Father Mark's stare is unwavering, like he's searching for something.

"Oh," I say, disappointed, and turn away.

"Look at me," Father Mark says, so I turn back. "As a career writer, I spend much of my time trying to read people, their characters, who they are behind the face and appearance. I'm always looking for interesting material. I can't help myself. After all these years I do it automatically, though I probably shouldn't. I suppose it's a bit invasive." He raises his glass to his lips, taking a small sip, holding it there. "When you walked into the school office—to get the news about your award—frankly, I was stunned."

"What . . . what do you mean?"

"I probably shouldn't say this, but the moment I first saw you, I wondered to myself: how did so much talent, such insight and imagination, come from a girl so young, and with such startling beauty? What a beauty! I thought. God must have extraordinary plans for such a creation as this."

"Oh. Um. Oh." I am embarrassed that he, too, this writer, this *priest*, would go *there*. "Well, you know . . . people always make the same assumptions, because . . . because of the way I look . . . people don't think I could be smart. They, um, they always act surprised like somehow it's weird or shocking which is so stupid. I hate it." As soon as the words are out I wish I could stuff them back in my mouth. "I'm sorry . . . I didn't mean to be rude or to insinuate . . . anything . . . I just . . . I must sound conceited . . . but . . ."

"Stop apologizing." Father Mark shakes his glass and the ice clinks. His elbow rests on the bar, so casual, so self-assured, the glass suspended in his hand, dangling there. The scotch is the same golden brown as his eyes. "It's classic, really. The curse of the pretty girl: everyone loves to look at her without trying to see what's inside. Perpetually underestimated. Am I right?"

I shrug my shoulders. The truth is, Father Mark says out loud what I would never admit.

"I'm still in the process of getting a read on you, Olivia Peters, and I am rather enjoying myself. You are an interesting study. I am eager to learn as much as I can about my beguiling new advisee. If you're not careful, you may find yourself in one of my stories." Father Mark chuckles, his eyes becoming world-weary for a brief moment. "Not to worry, though. I'd change your name and all significant identifying features." This provokes a bellow and Father Mark throws his head back and clutches a hand over his stomach.

I manage a laugh but begin to wonder how many drinks Father Mark had before I arrived.

"My apologies. You're here barely ten minutes and already I start on the advice and give away my dark secret that I'm not as nice as I appear, that sometimes I ingratiate myself just because a person might make a good character. Though, take it from me," he says, leaning toward me like he's about to reveal a secret. "Never forgo an opportunity to get to know someone who intrigues you."

I say nothing. I don't know what to say.

"But listen to me, talking nonstop, probably scaring you off—it's just the scotch speaking." The mention prompts him to take another sip. "Until now, writing has always been my first priority. As long as I keep producing even the Catholic Church lets me be. But this prize you won is meant to be my legacy, my plan to find the best young writers out there and give them their start. I want to offer you every resource I can. You'll have to be patient with me, though, I'm not used to dealing with young people with any regularity. I need a little trial and error period. How does that sound? Do we have a deal?"

"Sure. Yes." I force a smile, feeling a little awkward, and focus on his intentions, which are good.

"Now, enough about me. Let's talk about you. Your family. Your work. How you got into writing. Tell me everything."

"Um . . ." I tap my fingers on the bar, trying to figure out where to start. "So . . . my mom . . . she's a huge reader. Reads all the time and our house is packed floor to ceiling with books. And my father was . . . *is* . . ." I pause, not sure how to answer, "a book person, too. Though now, I don't know. Maybe not."

"He changed his mind?" Father Mark looks confused.

"No. Possibly." I pause and then just say it. "He left us. Ten years ago."

"I'm sorry to hear that."

"Life is better without him," I rush, wanting to move away from this topic. "Anyway, Mom brought my sister and me up reading just about everything you could imagine, including the American Catholic writers I mentioned earlier—my family is *really* Catholic." I shift in my chair, crossing one leg over the other, my fingers still tapping the edge of the bar. "Anyway, Mom has shelves filled with the Latin Americans, too. I'm trying to read in the original Spanish, now. It's slow going. But with the poetry especially, with someone like Pablo Neruda—his poems are nice in English but they are exquisite in Spanish."

"That's a very astute observation."

Father Mark stares into my eyes and I realize I am staring back and so I turn away, looking hard at the mug, sliding my hand around it, letting my skin feel the burn of the liquid, still hot inside.

"I can't really take credit."

"No?"

"I learned that from Mom. She's a purist when it comes to literature."

"You and your mother are close?"

"Yes. In fact, she's a writer, too. She's been writing mystery novels under a pen name since I was little. She'd kill me if I told you her pseudonym, though, and she doesn't like to talk much about her books as a general rule. We don't even have them on display in our living room. If you ever meet her don't tell her I mentioned it," I ramble on.

"Interesting. You are following in your mother's footsteps." Father Mark smiles, and then adds, conspiratorially, "Don't worry— I won't say a word. My lips are sealed." He sounds delighted that we share a little secret.

A spoon sits next to the mug and I plunge it into the hot chocolate, stirring it around to give myself something else to do, unsure how to act in this situation that is me sitting at a bar with someone famous who is paying me all sorts of attention, sitting so close, leaning even closer.

"So . . . um . . . thanks for reading one of my favorite stories," I continue, staring into the mug as the purply brown liquid swirls in circles even after I remove the spoon. "The Borges, I mean. That was really nice of you."

"Olivia." He draws out each syllable and again it sounds like music. Oh-liv-ee-aah.

"Yes?"

"Olivia," Father Mark repeats, and I look up from the mug, focusing on the endless bottles of liquor behind the bar.

"Look at me."

It's a request not an order. I shift toward Father Mark, body and eyes.

"No need to be embarrassed that you are precocious."

My eyes roll before I can stop them.

"I'm serious," he says, all playfulness gone. "You are different from most of your peers. You have promise. You are special. Your writing shows talent beyond your years. I am astounded by you, to be quite honest."

I blush. The warmth spreads all the way to the top of my forehead. Thoughts and questions fly through my mind. *He thinks I'm special. Different. How can he decide this from one story? After only a couple of interactions? Is there a magic formula? It can't be that easy . . . can it?*

"You shouldn't be shy about it," he continues. "I feel certain that success will come to you, Olivia. One day you will look back on this conversation and remember my prediction. I look forward to helping make it happen."

Wow, wow, wow, plays the soundtrack in my head. The red that's run all over my face continues over every inch of pale skin on my body to the tips of my fingers and toes.

"Okay. Enough embarrassment for today. It's your turn."

"My turn?"

"To ask questions. Anything you want."

"Like what?"

"Isn't there anything you are curious about?"

"Well . . ." My eyes flicker to the ceiling as they sometimes do when I am thinking about what to say next. The fans overhead turn, slow, and a shiver runs down my spine, reminding me of the cold. "When did you know you wanted to write? How old were you? Were you my age or younger or older?"

Father Mark seems pleased with my questions and begins to tell me how he was older than me, much older, late twenties and already a priest when he wrote his first novel—thirty the first time something was published. He explains how everything happened fast. That his first novel, *Hannah*, about the middle of three sisters who dies suddenly and leaves, quite literally, a hole between the older and younger sisters and how a family once strong can implode from this empty middle, became a best seller, and after *Hannah*, it all went very quickly, his writing career.

The conversation between us becomes easier now that it's his turn to open up, and the pace quickens once I am over feeling self-conscious and little-girlish about my Swiss Miss kid hot chocolate and my uniform skirt and socks. I have a lot of questions—no, a million—and Father Mark lets me ask every one though there is no way I can ask them all in a single afternoon. But I keep on and the discussion goes from somewhat awkward to beginning to seem normal to feeling like fire, like there is a spark and crackle and burning in the back-and-forth between us, and we talk and talk until finally I exclaim, "The time! What time is it?" as if I've been under a spell and forgotten where I am.

The bar is full now, teeming with people, but I hadn't noticed any of them arrive and so I imagine it must be late and it is.

"A little after seven," Father Mark says, checking his watch, and I gasp. "Don't worry, I'll drive you home," he says and I accept his nice offer, not even bothering to worry about all the scotch he's been drinking. Soon the check is paid and we are out the door and in his car, still talking, lobbing questions back and forth like we could go on this way forever, but before I know it I am out on the sidewalk in front of my house saying, "Thank you, thank you so much for the ride and everything today."

"I had a wonderful time, too, Olivia," Father Mark says, leaning across the passenger seat, looking at me through the open window. He is smiling. "Have a good night."

"You, too," I call out as his car pulls away, my hand raised in a wave. Only after it turns the corner, disappearing from sight, do I lower my arm. With a smile to match his, I float up the stairs and into the house on cloud nine.

ON SERENDIPITY

BY MORNING THE TEMPERATURE SHOOTS UP TO NINETY degrees and spring suddenly becomes summer in Boston, the humidity turning the air to liquid heat. Ash, Jada, and I go to Newbury Street to get ice cream after school. On the way we strip off our uniform socks and shoes and change into flip-flops. Ash and I grab a table inside the shop while Jada waits for the sundae we ordered to share.

"You were right. Eastern Standard is a bar," I admit. "But once I got over the initial awkwardness, and my total idiocy ordering hot chocolate, like I'm six years old or something—"

"You ordered hot chocolate at a bar? You should've asked for a real drink, something mature-sounding, like a Manhattan or a vodka on the rocks."

"That would've been a great idea, getting drunk with Father Mark."

"How can you even think of hot chocolate when it's a million degrees out?"

"It was freezing in there."

"What's this I'm hearing?" Jada places a dish piled high with ice cream, bananas, gooey caramel, and whipped cream in front of us and hands out napkins. "You and writer-priest-man drank hot chocolate together? How snow day of you."

"No. He had scotch." Just saying the word *scotch* like it's a normal part of my everyday conversation makes me feel sophisticated. "But that's not the point. The point is, even though it started out kind of weird, it ended up being really amazing. I mean, he's great to hang out with. I think we totally clicked, you know?" I stop a moment to eat a heaping spoonful of sundae, enjoying the cold relief on my mouth and throat. "We talked for hours and he told me all about his career and his life and how he finds stuff to write about and he let me ask anything I wanted."

"Did you ask him how to become famous?" Jada wants to know.

"I don't think he cares about fame."

"How can he not?"

"I don't think he gets out much, you know, because of all the writing."

"But he's on television and in the press constantly and doing readings like every other best-selling author in the universe," Ash says. "He gets out all the time."

"That's not what I meant."

"Say more then."

I try to find the right words. "Well, he is social in the ways you mentioned, but I think it's like, some sort of professional persona he adopts. In the end, he's pretty solitary—"

"Well he *is* a priest," Jada interrupts.

"But I think his solitude—at least if I'm understanding him right—has more to do with being a writer. He spent a lot of yesterday telling me to prepare myself for the loneliness that comes with writing, that it's inevitable, and even with success, after all is said and done there is only and always just you and the page." I do my best to affect his voice: a bit preachy, a little slurred. "That kind of stuff."

"Sounds dark," Ash says and pops a bite of banana into her mouth.

"Not exactly. More like, he's reached a point in life when, since he doesn't have children or a wife and he wants a legacy other than his books—he actually used that word when talking about the contest—he's thinking of the people who win this prize each year as his pseudo kids or something. Like, it's his job to take care of us. I don't know. Maybe I'm being overly analytical."

"Well," Ash says, "regardless of his reasons you get to be the beneficiary. Right place, right time. You know."

"And, on a different note . . ." Jada is ready to change the subject. "Guess what I have to report?"

"You heard from Sam, didn't you?" I exclaim, and when Jada nods I scold: "You waited an entire day of school to tell us?"

"I wanted to wait until we had time to discuss the intricacies of the conversation and examine it down to the very last detail."

"Given that neither Olivia nor I have a boy in our lives—not yet at least," Ash says, looking at me, mouthing the name Jamie, "we have all the time in the world to devote to your late-night exchange with Sam-u-el."

"So!" Jada seems ready to burst. "We IM'd for two hours last night," she begins, and for the next thirty minutes the three of us sit by the window, at our little metal table with the tiny, old-fashioned chairs, picking apart each word, fragment, and sentence of Jada's exchange with Sam, trying to figure out the meaning, however minuscule it might be.

"Maybe, once Sam and I fall madly in love—and Olivia and Jamie, or insert other college boy here, fall madly in love . . ." She gives me a look before continuing. "We can set you up with one of their friends." Jada reaches her hand across the table, tapping Ash's. "Because if Olivia and I end up with boyfriends then, of course, you will need one, too."

Jada is still talking about Sam when I notice two familiar people standing in front of the ice cream shop.

"Jada Ling!" I hiss. "I can't believe you."

"I might've sent a quick text on our way here," she sings, shooting me a sheepish look before she is up from her chair and out the door like a shot. I put my hands over my eyes, afraid to watch, afraid to be made a fool of, to act a fool, a jumble of nerves and thrills.

"What?" Ash asks, craning her neck to see whatever I'm seeing outside the window. "Who's out there?"

"Nobody," I say.

"That's a very hot nobody," Ash observes once she gets a good view.

Sam and Jamie—as in Jamie Grant—are locking up their mountain bikes to one of the meter poles along Newbury Street.

Jada knocks on the window, waving us to come outside.

"Go say hi to him already," Ash demands. "I'll watch our stuff. Besides, I don't want to be a third wheel."

"I can't." I am as frozen as the ice cream in our sundae.

"Olivia. Come on." She tries yanking me from my chair.

My shy side kicks into high gear, and when it's clear I'm not going anywhere, Ash takes matters into her own hands and before I can grab her she tells me, "Fine, you watch our stuff and I'll go get him for you."

Oh God, oh God, oh God, I repeat in my mind, then pull out the novel I've been reading, *The House of the Spirits* by Isabel Allende, to give myself something to do other than watch whatever is happening outside. But after I read the same paragraph over and over for what feels like five minutes, the door of the ice cream shop opens and I can't resist—I look up.

There. He. Is.

Jamie.

"Hi, Olivia," he says, walking over to the table. "Your friend Ashley said you might be getting lonely. Mind if I join you?"

Oh, Ash! "No, not at all," I say, grabbing my messenger bag off the seat and putting it on the floor to make room. "Of course not. Hi. Nice to see you again."

"Same here," he says, smiling, sitting down next to me, and I practically fall into his big dark eyes.

"Any luck getting into the class?" I ask, finally coming up with something to say, hopeful that the answer will be yes.

"Not yet. I'm getting there, though. Two signatures to go."

I think about whether or not I could help, whether I might have a little pull with Father Mark now that he and I have hung together in a bar, but then decide against suggesting this. "I'll keep my fingers crossed then," is what I tell him.

"I need all the help I can get," he says, laughing, playing with the tiny silver cross dangling from his neck, holding it out as if to say that prayer isn't out of the question, either.

"That's right. Selling your soul and all that. I remember."

There's a knock on the window. Sam gestures to Jamie that they need to go.

"I wish I had more time," he says.

Me, too, I think.

"We've got to go take our last exam in . . ." he pauses, pulling out his cell, "forty minutes. But before I go . . . I guess, I was wondering . . ."

He was wondering? Wondering what?

". . . if maybe we could, you know, exchange information. That way if I do get into the class, we could, I don't know, be in touch before it starts. I could give you my e-mail and number and get yours and then I'll know how to get ahold of you when I get the verdict."

"That would be great." I smile because it would be honestly, truly, utterly great. "I'd love that," I say. "I hope it works out. It would be fun to be in class together." An understatement.

He hands me his cell so I punch in my info and then I give him mine to do the same.

"So we'll be in touch," Jamie says, getting up. "Soon."

I sure hope so. More knocking on the window and I look out to see Sam, Jada, and Ash, hands cupped on the glass, watching us, smirking.

I will not turn red, I will not turn red.

"Sounds great," I say, glancing back at Jamie.

"Talk to you later then," he says and heads outside, holding the door for Jada and Ash to pass through.

"Bye, Jamie," they call.

"Now that wasn't so bad," Ash says, sitting down and diving back into what remains of our melted sundae. I am so jubilant that I can almost forgive her for being Ash, and Jada for setting me up. Jada is focused on scooping caramel out of the bottom of the dish, avoiding my eyes, but she can't contain the laughter bubbling up inside her. "You are shameless," I begin, when the door to the shop swings open again and my jaw drops and I think, *This cannot be happening, is this really, truly happening?*

"Olivia! I can't believe this," says a voice with genuine surprise.

"Wow. Hi, Father Mark." I stand up, a little unsteady.

"I was on my way to campus and it's so hot today I thought I'd treat myself."

"Father Mark, I want you to meet my two best friends, Ashley," I say, gesturing to Ash, "and Jada," who gives him a little wave. "They go to Sacred Heart, too." I'm reminded of my earlier comment about Father Mark being a lonely man. "Um, do you want to join us?"

A look that says, *Please no, don't do this to us*, appears on my friends' faces and then I realize that inviting Father Mark to join us is a bit weird, at least if you're not me and don't idolize him.

"You look like you're almost ready to leave." Father Mark hesitates, looking at the now empty sundae dish on the table, with barely a layer of melted ice cream at the bottom. But I can tell he'd like to accept the invitation.

"I was actually just going to order something else," I lie, but figure this gives him an excuse to sit with us awhile.

"Well, since you're so kind to offer, maybe I will stay for a few minutes." A smile lights up his face and eyes. He leans forward, hands clasped behind his back, and the medal of St. Benedict—his order of priests—dangles from his neck on a chain and shines when it catches the glare of the sun as it swings back and forth. He turns to Ash and Jada, who've gone silent. "Nice to meet you both. I'll be back in just a sec. Olivia, my treat. What would you like?"

"A small dish of the hazelnut, please."

"Do you girls want anything?"

"No thanks," Ash and Jada both say, and I glare at them for not accepting his friendly offer. Kick them under the table.

"It's the least I can do," he insists, pulling out his wallet.

"I'll try the coconut. Just one scoop, though," Ash relents, and I give her a look of gratitude. "Sugar cone, please," she adds.

"Me, too," Jada says, coming around. "Same."

"Good. Would you mind finding me a chair?"

I nod yes and drag one over from an empty table as Father Mark places everyone's orders at the counter.

"Olivia," Jada hisses, "why did you have to invite him to join us? It's awkward."

Ash looks more resigned than annoyed.

"Be nice. Please. This is important to me. Besides, he's nice. You'll see."

"You know he *is* pretty good-looking," Ash says. "For someone my dad's age."

"Can we not do this again?"

"Yeah, sorry. Just telling you what my eyes are telling me."

I shift in my seat. Avoid staring into anyone's eyes.

Father Mark has to make two trips between the table and the

counter. He brushes off our attempts to help, wanting to take care of everything himself, which is sweet. After asking Ash and Jada the basics, like have they lived in Boston all their lives, do they enjoy school at Sacred Heart, and what's their favorite subject, he asks them if they've read "The Girl in the Garden."

"Actually, yes we have," Ash says.

"You made an excellent choice," Jada informs him.

Father Mark smiles like a proud parent. "As soon as I finished it, I said to myself: this is it. This is the one!"

"Well, we think Olivia is pretty great, too." Ash grins, enjoying my embarrassment for the second time in a single hour.

"Yeah, we could tell you stories about Olivia."

"Like what? I'm curious." Father Mark leans toward Jada, eager to hear what she might reveal.

"Jada . . . *don't*," I warn.

"Like that Olivia has been valedictorian since practically our first day of high school."

"And honors night is like, the Olivia Peters show every year."

"*Ash . . .*"

They go back and forth, ignoring my plea, trading humiliating trivia about me to Father Mark who smiles and laughs over each new detail. If I wasn't so happy about everyone getting along, if I wasn't still aglow about Jamie getting my number and e-mail, I might mind even more, but I can tell this is my friends' way of getting comfortable around Father Mark, so I blush and bear it.

After a good ten minutes, though, I cut in, saying, "Okay, time's up. You two are worse than my mom."

Then, as if just remembering where he is, Father Mark jumps up from his chair. "You all have been so delightful, I almost forgot I was on my way to the university. I've got a To Do list a mile long," he says, looking at me. "I should dash."

"It's okay," I say. "Thanks for the ice cream."

"Nice to meet you," Ash says with sincerity as he gathers his things and smiles at each one of us before heading toward the door.

"Olivia," he says, holding it propped open, "we'll plan another get-together soon. If I don't run into you again first, of course," he adds with a laugh, and then he is gone.

This time, I don't doubt it.

ON SURPRISES

OVER THE NEXT COUPLE OF WEEKS, FATHER MARK BEGINS to schedule regular appointments to discuss the writing life, my story, revisions, no longer leaving any of our get-togethers to chance, and I am elated. One evening, after our fifth meeting— this one at a coffee shop—when I walk in the house, my mother is zipping around the kitchen and we are both so distracted we almost crash into each other. She has three pots going on the stove top, an apple half-chopped on a cutting board next to a pile of walnuts, a mixing bowl with a whisk sticking out, and the refrigerator door open wide.

"Whoa, Mom. Slow down. Can I help?"

Without a word she hands me the mixing bowl, and I start whisking what appears to be salad dressing. I've been meaning to tell her about the attention Father Mark has been paying me, how he's becoming a true mentor with an almost Dad-like interest in my well-being and success, but obviously now is not the right time so I don't mention it.

"After you finish with the dressing, get out the nice china bowl—it's on the top shelf of the cabinet. Throw in the arugula, walnuts, goat cheese, and pieces of apple and toss them together with the dressing." Mom wipes her forehead with the back of her hand. "Your sister and Luke will be here soon and I want everything perfect. Father MacKinley is coming, too."

"What's going on? You never stress out like this." I shut the fridge and set the dressing back on the counter so I can chop the rest of the apple. "Is everything okay?"

Mom smiles, stopping for a moment. "Better than okay."

I give her a look that says, *Tell me*, and feel a pang of guilt, worrying that lately I've been so caught up in my own world that I've missed something important.

"You'll know soon enough. Now finish making the salad." She lifts the lid off one of the pots on the stove, using a wooden spoon to stir whatever's inside.

"What are we having?" I ask, and Mom gives me a look that says I should know better. "Oh. Right. Fish." It's Friday, and in my family—especially if you are Greenie—fish isn't just something you eat during Lent.

Mom grabs my arm, stopping me for a moment. "Oh, Livvy. I hope you know I haven't forgotten about you."

"Me? What are you talking about?"

"I'm planning a more formal celebration, you know."

Oh. She means the contest. "You don't need to."

"But I want to host a big dinner, a special one, and have your friends over, Sister June, Father MacKinley, and I thought we would invite Father Mark, too." Mom smiles. "Do you think he'd come for dinner?"

"I think he'd love that, Mom." In fact, I know he would. "It would be great for you to meet him, too. You are a very nice mother." I lean over and kiss her on the cheek. "For now, though, let's just worry about getting this dinner ready that you're so stressed about."

"Yes. Right. I better start the fish since your sister likes it cooked to death." Mom turns on the burner under the grill pan. "I don't know how she eats fish that dry, but it's her night and I'm not going to interfere."

After the salad is ready, I set the table in the dining room and put out wine glasses by each of the place settings, lighting the candles in the center as a finishing touch. Once we dim the lights, the room will look perfect.

As I survey my work, straightening the silverware, I wonder what's so special about this evening, if maybe Greenie and Luke are more serious than I realized. Back in January, Luke actually came over to ask Mom's permission to take Greenie on a first date. It was kind of sweet. Mom said yes—like she was going to say no—so Greenie and Luke started going on chaperoned dates. They haven't even kissed yet. Greenie says she isn't kissing anyone until she's engaged. She wants the only boy she's ever kissed to be the one she marries. Luke feels the same way. I wish they would get on with it already since I don't want to be the only sister kissing college boys—well, if it eventually comes to that. Greenie's friends at HMU are just like her—it's all part of being a good Catholic apparently, at least in her world.

"Olivia," Mom calls from the kitchen. "Can you come here and check on the soup? I've got to deal with these carrots."

"Coming!" I grab the matches off the table so I can put them away. "Don't you think it's a little hot outside for soup, Mom?"

"Well, who knew it was going to go up into the nineties so

soon," she says, removing the steamer filled with carrots from the pot. "But I made this soup the very first time that Luke came for dinner so I don't care if it's the hottest day of the year—we're having it."

"Okay, whatever you say."

"So tell me, sweetie," Mom says, tipping the carrots into a bowl, steam rising up around her face, "how does it feel to have your writing gain the approval of a famous novelist? I've always said you have talent."

"Exciting. Surreal. I even got to hang out with Father Mark after school today." I drop this like it's totally normal.

"You were out with Father Mark! Olivia, how wonderful."

"We've been meeting to do edits on my story."

"That's a big deal, having someone like him take time out from his schedule to focus on you. I'm so proud."

"He's just being nice, Mom."

"Well, I hope I get to meet him soon. I have to admit, I'm a little jealous of you," she says, chuckling.

The front door creaks and the sound of voices floats from the foyer into the kitchen. "That must be your sister and Luke. Hurry!" Mom rips off her apron, hanging it on the hook. She fluffs her bangs. "Do I look all right?"

"Great, as always, Mom," I respond, but she is already on her way out of the kitchen so I hurry to follow her.

Greenie stands in the foyer, Luke behind her, his hands on her shoulders. Greenie and Luke are the picture-perfect couple—blond hair, blue eyes. Luke towers over Greenie's tiny frame, even with her ballerina posture.

"Hi, Mom. Hi, Olivia," she says, and I can feel her nervous excitement fill the room.

"Hey, you." I say, next in line to give her a hug after Mom. "Greenie . . . you look . . . I don't know. Overjoyed?" Then I notice Mom's face is almost as aglow as my sister's.

Greenie whips her pale, slender arm from behind her back. A tiny round diamond sparkles on the ring finger of her left hand and I gasp.

"I asked Greenie to marry me and she said yes," Luke says, happier than I've ever seen him.

"Congratulations!" I squeeze my sister into another hug, the biggest I can manage. Getting married at twenty-one is young, but among Greenie's friends, it's typical. "Does that mean you guys finally kissed?" I whisper in Greenie's ear. When I pull back her face is so red she doesn't need to say a word. "You and I will discuss *that* later," I mouth and she nods.

Tears pour down Mom's face. The doorbell rings. "That must be Father MacKinley," she says, and Luke goes to let him in.

"You knew, didn't you?" I say to Mom as she dabs her eyes with a tissue. "Of course you knew."

Mom nods her head, guilty as charged.

"Let me see that ring again," I demand, and Greenie offers her hand. "It's beautiful," I say, admiring the setting.

"You'll be my maid of honor, won't you?"

"Of course. I'll wear anything you want, even if it's hideous. Oooh! We get to go wedding dress shopping."

"I know," Greenie says, and her face lights up even more.

Luke reappears and we turn to greet Father MacKinley, but

Luke's alone and wearing a strange expression on his face. "Olivia," he says, "you have a visitor. Waiting out front."

"I'm not expecting anyone," I say, caught off guard, still focused on the wedding planning I'm going to do with Greenie.

"It's Father Mark Brendan," he informs me, sounding serious. "He says he has something important for you."

"Oh. Wow. He's here now?" My cheeks flush.

"Yes. Standing outside."

"Luke, you should have invited him in," my mother says, but I can tell she's flustered by our surprise guest.

"I did, but he said he didn't want to intrude. I also told him that we, well, that Olivia was in the middle of celebrating a special occasion." Luke stands there looking awkward, and I realize I need to do something to diffuse the strange feeling that has settled on the room, interrupting Greenie and Luke's big announcement.

"I'll go see what he wants. I'll only be a minute and then we can get on with dinner," I say, anxious to ease the tension.

"Well, I want to meet him," Mom says, recovering her composure. "Maybe we should see if he wants to stay. Greenie, Luke, you wouldn't mind, would you?"

"The more the merrier," Greenie says, being her usual generous self.

"Olivia," Mom beckons, heading into the foyer with me stumbling behind her, trying to catch up. The front door is wide open. Father Mark stands there on our stoop, tall, imposing all in black. "Well hello, Father." My mom rushes up. "I'm Marcela Peters, Olivia's mother." Mom extends her hand, which he clasps, pulling her forward to give her a kiss on the cheek, which I can tell startles her, but then she laughs.

"It's wonderful to meet you," Father Mark says, letting go. "I'm sorry to show up unannounced, but I have something for Olivia that didn't want to wait. I meant for you to take this home when you left the coffee shop," he says, turning to me, "but we were so lost in conversation that I forgot."

"Hi, Father," I say, feeling shy standing next to my mother.

He nods, opening his bag, and removes a manila envelope. "Here they are—the comments we discussed and the letter explaining the more substantial changes I suggested."

I take the envelope from his hand. "Thank you."

"Please, come inside. It's sweltering." Mom tries to coax him into the house. "We'd love for you to have dinner with us. I've been meaning to plan a special night to celebrate Olivia's news, actually."

"That's very nice of you, but I only had a minute and thought I'd drop this by since I was in the area."

"Are you sure?" Mom is hesitant to let him leave. "You'll come for dinner another night then?"

"Absolutely. I look forward to it," he replies. Father Mark is about to say something else when Father MacKinley arrives at our front steps.

"Mark," he exclaims. "What are you doing here?" They shake hands. Father MacKinley glances from Father Mark to me and makes the connection. "Oh, that's right. Olivia. How wonderful. Are you here for dinner, too?" he asks.

"No, I was just leaving," Father Mark responds, turning to go. "I don't want to keep you from your evening plans any longer."

"Where's the happy couple?" I hear Father MacKinley whisper to my mother.

"The dining room," she answers, and he heads inside, calling out over his shoulder, "See you later, Mark."

I stand there, holding the envelope, wanting to open it but knowing I have to wait, that it would be rude to take up any more of Greenie and Luke's celebration time. "Bye, Father Mark," I say, watching him walk toward the street and turn onto the sidewalk out front.

"Have a good night, Olivia," he replies, stopping for a moment. "It was lovely to meet you, Ms. Peters."

"Please, call me Marcela."

"Marcela," he says with a smile, and continues on his way.

When Mom shuts the door I can no longer tell if her glow is from Greenie's announcement or from meeting Father Mark. "Well, that was lovely!" Her cheeks are flushed, her eyes bright. "Okay," she says, more to herself than me. "Back to the engagement dinner." I follow her into the dining room, stashing the envelope in a stack of papers on a table in the hall. We resume our evening as if there was no interruption, as if Father Mark Brendan, the famous writer, didn't just show up on our doorstep to give me edits, like this is something that happens all the time.

"Let's make a toast," Mom says, picking up the crystal glass by her place at the table. "To Greenie and Luke on your engagement."

"To Greenie and Luke," Father MacKinley and I echo, and everyone clinks glasses, erupting into chatter about wedding dates and plans and guest lists and how, of course, Father MacKinley will say the wedding, and I try to stay focused. But the envelope waiting for me in the hall is tugging at my consciousness, pulling on my attention. When Greenie asks if something is wrong and

Luke says I seem distracted, I push thoughts of the envelope and its contents away and say, "Everything is wonderful. The best ever!" with enthusiasm, and determine to give myself over to Greenie's happy news. For now I let it go because there will be time to read later and I have seeing Father Mark again to look forward to as well. I am sure of this now. After these last few weeks, why wouldn't I be?

ON AN EMBARRASSMENT
OF RICHES

WHEN I ARRIVE AT SCHOOL THE FOLLOWING MONDAY A package is waiting for me in the office. I tear open the brown paper, right there at the counter, and gasp. Inside are two books, slim volumes. One is *Hannah*, by Mark D. Brendan, a first edition with the inscription *To Olivia Peters, I look forward to reading your first novel and wanted you to have a special copy of mine, Yours, Mark*, on the title page. The other is *A Good Man Is Hard to Find and Other Stories*, by Flannery O'Connor, signed by the author. I pick them up, turn them around, look at them from every angle. I feel like I should handle them with gloves. The O'Connor must be worth a fortune.

"That's quite a gift," Sister June says over my shoulder. "May I have a look?"

"Of course," I say, making room for her at the counter.

She opens each one and then reads the dedication inside *Hannah*, and for some reason my cheeks begin to burn. "You've made quite an impression on Father Mark." There is kindness in her eyes, but something else, too, something I can't quite put my finger on. She hands the books back. "Take good care of these," she says, and walks into her office, shutting the door behind her.

A note slips out from between the pages of the O'Connor.

> *Dear Olivia,*
>
> *I came across <u>A Good Man Is Hard to Find</u> at a rare books shop over the weekend and thought of you. I couldn't resist. Your youthful energy and enthusiasm is infectious. I am getting more pleasure out of spending time with you than I ever would have dreamed. Consider this a small thank-you and I hope I am not presumptuous giving you my first novel in the hope that it might inspire you.*

He's thanking *me*? This strikes me as incredible. And this gift is not small at all.

The note is signed:

> *Until next time,*
> *Mark*

By now I know that *next time* means soon, maybe even today, and so when Father Mark is waiting outside the school entrance after the final bell, wanting to see if I like the books—yes, of course I do, I tell him—and asking do I also want to go for coffee? I am not that surprised by the invitation or his presence and say yes. And then, there is not only this next time for coffee but another next time for dinner later in the week and another next time for lunch the following weekend. Soon there are too many next times to count and each new day has me waking up wondering, *What else will he bring me, give me, ask me to do now?* A letter tucked inside my locker, a card slipped under our front door, an envelope filled with poems by Stephen Dunn—*Do you know him?* Father Mark's note inquires—left at the school reception desk and my name called over the intercom, "Olivia Peters, would you please come to the office? You have another package."

Another package.

By the beginning of June I've learned to walk to the rhythm Father Mark sets without too much thought. I just follow along, the harmony to his melody. He is a warm weather Secret Santa who showers me with possibilities, commentary, invitations, literature. When, before I can blink, the school year is almost at an end and his attention still shows no sign of abating, I don't know what to make of it, what to think of it, so I don't think at all.

I just do, do, *do.*

One day I return home to find my mother drinking her afternoon chamomile tea in the living room, like always, but then, not at all like always because she is drinking her tea and chatting with Father Mark and not Father MacKinley.

Another impromptu visit to our house, not that I am keeping count.

"Olivia!" she says, smiling, when she sees me hovering in the hall, trying to get over my surprise at seeing her and Father Mark talking like old friends. "I told Father you'd be home soon."

"Hello," Father Mark says, leaning forward, his teacup clinking against the saucer, his eyes sparkling.

"Hey," I say, and walk over to the couch, sitting down on the opposite end from my mother.

"Would you like some tea?" she asks.

"Sure," I respond because I figure, why not? Why not have afternoon tea with Father Mark and my mother in our living room as if it is something we do together every day?

"Father Mark and I were just discussing his seminar," Mom says, seeming pleased by this. She gets up to grab another cup and saucer from the china cabinet and pours me some tea and another cup for herself.

"I can't wait for the class to start," I say, and Father Mark nods, smiles, because it is his class that I am referring to again as *the* class as if there is no other. "The end of June feels so far away, though. I still have to get through my last week of school."

"You'll make it." My mother sinks back onto the couch, getting comfortable, and the three of us spend the next hour chatting about this and that, Greenie's wedding, my story, Mom's novels—Father Mark presses her to reveal her pseudonym—she doesn't, but is clearly flattered by his interest and even engages him in a discussion about building suspense when writing a mystery.

Eventually we say our goodbyes—"See you soon, Olivia," he says, like always, before leaving, and I nod yes, like always, because we have a pattern now, after so many exchanges—then go upstairs, my mind racing, working overtime, thinking about how I never say no to Father Mark. I go to everything he invites me to, do everything he asks of me, read everything he recommends, as if it's my new full-time occupation, becoming all mentored and improved and approved by him, so much so that lately I almost can't find time to do anything else, see anyone else. I tear around my bedroom, gathering everything tangible—the notes, the books, the articles torn from magazines and the newspaper, the ticket stubs, manuscript drafts—and pile them together on my coffee table, the spoils of so much obedience. I am tempted to count everything, wishing that I could add the phone calls, the e-mails, and the texts to the pile, too—who knew that priests sent text messages?—as if somehow everything before me can quantify my worth, my potential, *all that he sees in me.* Instead I sift through the remnants of the last six weeks to remind myself that it is real.

I glow and bask and shine. So much I might burst.

Sitting cross-legged on my couch, I open my laptop and let my fingers fly. I am inspired. My thoughts are flickers of fire that become words on the screen and a new story and I type, type, type until I have emptied all the words streaming through my mind, until there are none left, and then set the screen to Sleep.

I call the story "Lucky."

I will show "Lucky" to Father Mark tomorrow.

I hope he likes it.

Then my thoughts flicker to Jamie. If only Jamie would be in touch like he promised then life would be perfect. Jada says to be patient, but it's been ages since that day we exchanged info. I close my laptop and set it down next to me and sigh, telling myself I really have nothing to complain about.

Piece by piece, I move the pile on the coffee table to the corner of my room, between the couch and the window, with letters and notes in one neat, tall stack, articles in another, again feeling pleased to have such a wealth of keepsakes, to be made so rich by someone who, I have to admit, I've noticed barely gives others the time of day. Well, unless they are somehow related to me.

Later that night, after I shut off the light and get into bed, I thank God for sending me yet another Father, the best, most interesting, supportive one a girl could ask for. The gratitude, the grace I feel from having Father Mark in my life stays with me, comforts me, as I drift off to sleep and dreams.

✤ I I ✤

And now I fear that a chain of events has started
that cannot be stopped.

—THOMAS MERTON

ON DISAPPEARANCES

"WHERE HAVE YOU BEEN?" ASH IS LEANING AGAINST MY locker when I arrive on our last day of school, arms crossed, her mouth gathered into a pout, but I can't tell if she is angry for real.

"Paris, darling," I drawl, trying to lighten the mood, and a tiny smile appears on Ash's face. I drop my bag at her feet. "Move over," I tell her. "I need to clean this out before the final bell."

"Nope," she says, shaking her head. "Not until we have a serious discussion about your recent disappearances."

"Disappearances?" My eyebrows arch with surprise but I already know what is coming. I've been waiting for it. Preparing.

"Jada," Ash calls out. "Over here!"

"Come on, Ash, move over," I plead.

"Sorry." She lays her arms out against the lockers as if they need protection.

"Is that—could it be—*no*—I think it's . . . it's . . . Olivia Peters!" Jada says, approaching us, her hair pulled up in two high pigtails clasped with plastic rainbow disks that somehow make her both beautiful and cute. She squeezes in next to Ash against my locker and proclaims, "This is an intervention, sugar pie. Where have you been hiding?"

"An intervention? Why do I need an intervention?"

"You wouldn't if you returned our texts and calls and IM's," Jada explains.

Here we go.

"I've been really busy—you know, wedding planning and . . ." I try to think of another excuse but come up short, forgetting all the ones I'd lined up for this very occasion. Though it's true wedding plans take up almost all my non–Father Mark time now.

"Yeah. And? So?" Jada snaps the gum she is chewing. "We couldn't tag along and help?"

"I'm the maid of honor," I protest.

"Since when has spending time with your sister excluded spending time with us?" Ash demands.

"And since when is wedding planning a full-time job?"

All good questions.

"Still waiting for an answer." Jada snaps her gum again.

"We're worried about where you've been and why you keep ditching us."

"Okay. Fine. If you want to know the truth—"

"We do," Ash says, matter-of-fact.

"Aside from wedding stuff, I've been working on my story revisions, like all the time," I explain, but leave the part about Father Mark's presence out, though I'm not quite sure why since I usually tell Ash and Jada everything down to the last detail. "It's going to be published so, you know . . . it's really important I get it done."

"Right." Jada's mouth is open, about to say something else, when Sister June appears out of nowhere, a tissue in her hand.

"Ms. Ling," she says. "Spit it out now."

"Sorry, Sister June." Jada's eyes widen with regret and her body slumps. "Does this mean I have detention?"

Sister June hides a smile, trying to maintain a strict demeanor. "No, Ms. Ling. I'm not without a heart you know," she says, wrapping the tissue around Jada's gum and handing it back to her. "I don't give out detentions on the last day of school. Now go throw this out before I change my mind," she adds, walking over to another group of girls who are squealing about something or other and telling them to lower their voices.

"Are you mad at us?" Jada asks.

"Is there something we did? Or didn't do?" Ash wants to know.

"I am not mad at either of you. Just busy. Busier than usual." Guilt hits me like a truck and I suddenly feel like a bad person for neglecting them. "If it makes you feel any better, I've missed hanging out."

"So you don't hate us?"

"Of course not. Stop saying that," I plead and my insides swim with guilt. "Can we start this conversation over? I promise to be a better friend from this moment forward." I give them my best puppy dog eyes. "Please?"

"Well. Okay. I guess we can try and restart our morning," Jada says, looking over at Ash for confirmation, and she nods her head yes.

Ash offers a suggestion: "I'd begin by asking Jada the following: Jada, are you and Sam in love?"

"That's such an exaggeration." Jada fidgets, pulling her hair out of her pigtails, letting it fall down to the middle of her back, parting it and then gathering it back up into the two clips. "It's only been like a few weeks and we've only gone out, officially, twice. So far," she adds.

"You went out? Like on a date," I say, disbelieving that I'm that out of touch with my friends and missing out on major news.

"Dinner and a movie," she says, triumphant. "And a picnic one afternoon in the park."

"Tell me as many details as possible before the bell rings."

"It's really not a big deal," Jada says, but her eyes fill with excitement and she looks like she might burst if she holds back any longer. "Though we've been talking every night on the phone and IM. And just so you know, Jamie—"

My ears perk up at the mention of Jamie's name.

"—is planning on—"

Just then, my cell rings, interrupting Jada.

Damn.

"You're going to answer it, aren't you?" Jada's disappointment is plain. "Is that going to be Greenie about more wedding stuff?"

"Oh, it's probably Father Mark." Ash looks annoyed and I am startled by her good guess.

"Come on. Cut me a break." Feeling self-conscious and embarrassed, I dig out my phone, looking around to make sure there aren't any teachers nearby, and flip it open.

"Hi, Olivia, it's Mark," says the voice on the other end.

"Hi, Father Mark."

Jada and Ash groan, mouthing, "Told you," to each other.

"Hang on," I tell him. "I need to take this," I say to Ash and

Jada, but a frost has already settled again between us. "I thought you guys liked him. This is important. Please be understanding. *Please.*"

"What else do you think we've been lately, Olivia?" Ash says, and she and Jada stalk off.

I feel deflated. Tired. Reluctant. "Hello," I say into the receiver.

"Olivia? Did you hear me? It's Mark."

"I know. How are you?" I still can't bring myself to call him Mark even though that's how he always refers to himself. It seems wrong, like calling my friends' parents by their first names. But it seems especially wrong to leave off "Father" with a priest.

I just wasn't raised that way.

"Why don't you come by my office hours after school," he suggests, though it's not really a suggestion. By now he assumes that whatever he asks of me, I'll do, because, well, I always do what he wants.

"Um . . ." I hesitate. For the first time I feel the urge to say no, not only because Ash and Jada will be disappointed, more so than they are already, but because we always celebrate the last day of school together and I don't want to miss out. Giving this afternoon to Father Mark instead of my friends seems not quite right. Seventeen-year-old girls like me should be hanging out, gossiping about boys with their two best friends, and not spending all their time with priests.

"Olivia," he presses, and I hear an impatient sigh.

"Well . . ."

All you need to do is say no, I tell myself. Just say it: *No. I have other plans, Father Mark. I'll see you another time.*

"Olivia."

But maybe he won't be fine. What if he isn't? What if he gets mad?

"Okay," I agree, after a long silence. "I'll be there at three-thirty." I guess I won't be mending fences with Ash and Jada today after all.

"Great, Olivia," he says with a trace of relief. "See you soon then."

"Bye, Father Mark," I say, and press the End button.

I look around the hall, but Jada and Ash are long gone, so I head to the cafeteria for my free period. The place is empty, with everyone in class or the library or wherever else people hide during study hall on the last day of school. My fingers work the clasp of my messenger bag and I flip it open, pulling out my laptop, setting it on a table. If I am going to be alone, if I am going to be all writerly like Father Mark says I am, then I might as well act the part. I put my fingers on the keyboard and wait. I wait and wait, but for the first time in ages nothing happens. Nothing comes. I feel stuck, stuck thinking about Ash and Jada's frustration with me, stuck ruminating on why I haven't yet heard from Jamie and why, for that matter, I hear from Father Mark so much. No words flow into my hands and this makes me feel not just alone but lonely and I wonder if this is the beginning of the isolation Father Mark so often talks about. As the minutes tick by I feel worse and more than ever like a bad friend. But if Ash and Jada are real friends, they'll get over it eventually, they'll see that I'm only doing what's best, taking advantage of opportunities while I still have the chance, since I'm sure, I'm *positive*, that this can't last forever.

ON CRUSHES

THE AFTERNOON IS BEAUTIFUL AND BRIGHT, AND AS I stroll down the hall toward Father Mark's office I wonder again why I am about to spend the first few official hours of summer laboring over story edits instead of enjoying the weather and freedom. For a short moment, this contest and all it has brought feels like a chain around my neck, a leash keeping me tied somewhere inside Father Mark's orbit, which seems just short of everyone else's. These thoughts dissipate, though, when I knock on his door, which stands ajar because he is expecting me, and when he calls out "Enter," I walk in like I own the place, sitting down on the smooth leather couch like I am well accustomed to being here, because I am.

"How are you today, Olivia?" Father Mark looks up from his desk.

"A little tired," I admit, watching as he finishes up whatever he is doing on the computer and comes over to sit down next to me. As usual, the manuscript is already set out on the coffee table and he picks it up, looking at me.

"Am I working you too hard?"

"No, no. Not at all." I smile to reassure him.

"Ready?"

"Sure," I say, reminding myself what a privilege it is to be here.

His office—the first time I saw it I gasped—stands out like a prize alongside those of his colleagues in the HMU English department. It shouts, "I am important! I have done great things to deserve a place like this!" With its tall bay window overlooking the Charles River and a mammoth desk, it's a regular palace. Paintings hang on every available wall space not taken up by bookshelves—he has more books than anyone I know, even my mother. A fireplace—unlit now, of course—is built into one side of the room, with a couch and matching chairs arranged like a sitting area in front of it.

Sunlight streams in and falls across everything. Over Father Mark and me.

We sit side by side, leaning forward over the coffee table, slightly tilted toward each other, both of us poring over my manuscript. I am listening intently to Father Mark's tips on plotting the short story when someone else walks in. There is barely time to register the eyes, the hair, the perfect-fitting jeans, the way he moves, before the name *Jamie Grant* flashes in my mind alongside the thought *You are beautiful*, and it takes everything in my power to resist asking him, *Why haven't you been in touch? You said you would be.*

He doesn't notice me at first, but when he does I can tell he is surprised and that he wants to smile, in fact, his eyes are smiling and he blinks them in this way that says, *Hello, how nice to run into you again*, which sparks joy to run right across my face. I can't hold it back. He is close enough that I can hear his breath come in quick, short bursts, see the dark center of his eyes, notice his long eyelashes, take in the musculature of his hands, fingers that grasp a single sheet of paper.

That's when I know why he's here.

Jamie waits for Father Mark to acknowledge him, breaking the hold his eyes have on mine, glancing out the windows and then, nervously, back at Father Mark, who hasn't yet said a word, whose eyes are focused on me even though my attention keeps flickering away to Jamie because I can't help myself and because I begin thinking, *Father Mark is being rude.* As this thought flashes through my mind I realize somehow that to Father Mark, Jamie is not a visitor but an intruder.

And next . . . next I wonder whether I have some bit of power to fix this awkward situation, that maybe if I acknowledge Jamie, then Father Mark will, too, and the hostile feeling emanating from him will disappear because Father Mark listens to me—he pays attention to what I think as if it's the most important thing he has ever heard in his life.

I clear my throat, shift my eyes from Jamie to Father Mark and back.

"Hi," I say to Jamie.

"Hi, Olivia," Jamie responds, polite, but looking away, as if he intuits somehow not to pursue any further conversation with me at this particular moment, as if it would upset Father Mark and then he would have to leave without the precious signature for which he came.

I wait for Father Mark to say hello back, to break the silence that has fallen over the room, but this does not happen. Father

Mark says nothing. Instead we are left in a strange, tense triangle—Father Mark's unwavering eyes on me, on my face. Jamie's eyes, here, there, everywhere—awkward, nervous. My eyes on Jamie's, unabashed, focused, riveted.

"Do you need something?" Father Mark barks, angry, twisting away from me toward Jamie like the sharp snap of a tree branch. "Can't you see I'm busy?"

"Sorry," he mutters. He holds the paper out.

There is another long pause before Father Mark grabs it, signs the form without even reading it, and hands it back, and before I can blink Jamie is gone. Poof. Out the door and out of my sight yet again with no other sign or encouraging word that tells me whether or not he'll ever be in touch like he said.

Before Father Mark returns to whatever wisdom he was about to offer me, his ever-willing supplicant, on the plotting of the short story, I blurt, "So do you know Jamie Grant?" I do nothing to hide the enthusiasm and interest in my voice because I assume Father Mark will get a kick out of the fact that I have a crush and because I am also imagining that this revelation might break the ice, that I can be the schoolgirl with a crush and suddenly Father Mark will laugh an appropriately fatherly laugh and give me advice about college boys like I am his daughter, feeling protective and expressing concern about the fickle boys who attend his university, like any other father who is not also a Father would.

I assume wrong.

And right away I know I've made a mistake. A grave error. Misread the situation. I am wrong to think that talking about this visitor—this intruder—is a good idea, a laugh-inducing, situation-fixing move.

Father Mark's body stiffens, his mouth clamps shut, his face pales. I detect more than a trace of anger in his eyes before he can mask it, which tells me I've overstepped a boundary, some unmarked, invisible boundary, a half-buried mine that I should have known was there, about to explode. Yet I also have no way of knowing, because where are the boundaries between Father Mark and me?—other than the usual mentor-student ones, which so far seem to involve give, give, give on Father Mark's part and take, take, take on mine, and this thought calls to mind the ever-growing pile between the couch and the windowsill in my room, the collection of mementos that is my proof, my evidence that I mean something to Father Mark, that I am his legacy like he always says.

Guilt thunders through me at the possibility that I have somehow violated this man's generosity, profaned his charitable impulses by introducing something as base and vulgar as a crush. I feel like a child who has just walked into church wearing a bathing suit, dripping wet, flip-flopping down the center aisle, sand caked to my chubby kid ankles and legs and leaving a trail behind me.

Everything, me, suddenly, I am all wrong.

I should never have made the kind of comment I would make to Ash or Jada or Greenie to Father Mark, who I must remember—even though lately it is harder and harder to remember—is not a friend or sister like they are. He is a famous writer and a respected professor and a priest, for God's sake. I can't believe I'd be so dumb as to try and chat with him about a cute boy. No matter how talented he thinks I am I bet all he sees now is a silly high school student sitting beside him, her face burning with embarrassment.

I never find out what Father Mark is thinking, though, because after this moment of silence that falls like a hammer between us and feels like forever, he recovers and goes right back to discussing plotting as if nothing interrupted us. Nothing at all.

"You need to move the story forward at a faster pace here," he says, leaning over, leaning toward me, pointing to a paragraph on the page he holds out. His forearm, exposed, the long-sleeved black shirt of a priest rolled up to his elbows, brushes my skin and I will myself to be still, not to move a muscle, not to flinch or shrink back. "You should cut all of this." His other hand slices across the paper like a knife.

I pretend I'm paying attention, but my mind is stuck mucking around in the swamp of all this unease and I find myself wishing Father Mark would have just laughed it off, turned the situation into a joke, or even just answered the question and told me what he knew about Jamie, if anything, and moved on from there. That would have been less awkward. At least for me.

I am also wishing his skin, his priest's arm, would stop touching mine.

"Olivia? Olivia!" Father Mark demands my attention. He realizes I'm not focused. My skin is on fire. I can almost hear it crackling.

"I'm so sorry," I say, banishing all other thoughts as I lean toward Father Mark to look intently at the page between us, letting my arm push more forcefully against his, as if this will somehow diffuse the strangeness, as if my arm and his pressed together will help him forgive my trespasses, as if trespassing into his personal space is the answer to diffusing whatever has just transpired, though what it is, I do not know for sure. "You were saying . . ."

We eventually get back on track as we sit there together on his important couch in his important office, and soon he even praises something in the manuscript and I smile, grateful and relieved that he still thinks I am a good writer, a good girl, that I have potential, that we have recovered that rhythm, the rapport that's been so easy, so obvious between us from the very first moment we met.

Almost. We almost get back to it.

"I'll see you in class, Olivia," Father Mark says when we've finished and I am on my way out, my hand already on the door, and I freeze.

"Yes," I reply, feeling startled, hurt even, turning back one last time to look at him, both of us fully aware that in this short statement he's declared a two-week break in what has become our daily interaction as if it's totally normal and not at all a big deal when it seems like a very big deal to me given everything, given the last month and a half and his near constant attention. But he is smiling so I return the smile, I force a smile when I add "I can't wait" and "See you in a couple of weeks then," before I walk through the door and turn down the shadowy hallway, my steps zigzagging this way and that because in truth I am thrown a little off-balance.

ON FEELING WOUNDED

ON THE WAY HOME FROM FATHER MARK'S OFFICE I WORK away at my surprise about his sudden change in attitude until it's almost gone, like cleaning out a cut and covering it with a Band-Aid so it doesn't get infected. I text Jada and Ash to make plans for every night the rest of this week since my new plan is to squeeze as much girlfriend time as possible into what I imagine is a temporary suspension of Father Mark–Olivia time, turning it into something good. Making the best of a sad situation and all that. Within minutes we decide to go to the movies tomorrow night and maybe out for dinner on Thursday, and I am grateful that Jada and Ash are not the type to hold a grudge. Next I text Greenie about going wedding dress shopping this Saturday and soon she and I agree to meet on Newbury Street at 10 a.m. The memory of how I filled my evenings and weekends before Father Mark gets stronger, and after a few tentative pedals and some wobbles I am off and speeding steadily.

Then something exciting and unexpected happens and helps me make an almost full recovery. *Ping* goes my cell and it lights up with the name *Jamie Grant*. I have a text.

So I'm officially IN Father Mark's class. You free later? Want to get coffee and celebrate?

I do my best to skip over the mention of Father Mark and text, Yes, I am free, in fact 2 day was our last day of school, back to Jamie with my heart doing a happy dance the entire time it takes me to punch in the message and until the very moment another *ping* sounds on my cell.

How's 6pm? Trident Cafe on Newbury? Jamie wants to know.

I'll be there. CU then, I respond and hurry home to change out of my uniform, running upstairs to my bedroom without pausing to say hi to Mom who is tucked away working in her study. Whenever she starts a new novel the rule in our house is that, barring emergencies like someone losing a limb and/or bleeding profusely, she'll come to us when she's ready and not the other way around.

Moving dress by dress through my closet, I search for the right outfit to wear for my maybe-date with Jamie—*maybe* because I am unsure about whether getting coffee counts officially as a date. When my eyes land on the baby blue shift dress I bought back in April at my favorite vintage haunt I yank it from the hanger and pull it over my head and know immediately it's the right choice for a warm summer's evening—pretty and casual yet not so casual that it says *I don't care.* The delicate fabric feels smooth against my skin. I slip on a pair of platform sandals and stare at my reflection in the mirror.

It'll do.

I complete the look with lipstick and grab my shoulder bag to head out because Trident Cafe is a bit of a walk and I don't want to be late.

Mom stands by the front door, sorting the mail. She has emerged for the evening.

"Hi, Mom," I say, and smile. "How's the new novel coming?"

"Oh. You know. Hard to tell at this stage. Still working through the mystery part."

"I'm sure you'll figure it out. You always do."

"You look so pretty, Olivia." She sounds surprised.

"Thank you," I say, turning to catch my reflection in the long mirror in the foyer.

"Is it me," Mom begins, thoughtful. "Or has Greenie convinced you to go on some sort of fashion fast recently? I haven't seen you dressed like this in weeks and, correct me if I'm wrong, but usually the second warm weather hits Boston you are out of your uniform and into a sundress and sandals after school as much as humanly possible."

The eyes looking back at me in the mirror change from carefree to uncomfortable as I consider my mother's observation. Hanging out with a priest on a regular basis doesn't exactly inspire a girl to dress to impress, so lately I just . . . well . . . I haven't been my typical, summer-obsessed self. But then, is there anything typical about life since the day I met Father Mark? And besides, wouldn't it be weird if I was meeting up with him looking like I do now, like I am about to go on a date, or in something I would wear to hang out with Ash and Jada?

"I think you're just imagining things, Mom" is my answer, and I reach for the door but find out she has yet another question before she's going to let me go.

"Maybe. But, do I detect a special occasion behind this outfit? Is there a boy involved?"

A smile tugs at my lips.

"There *is* a boy." Mom gets excited. "Where does he go to school? Have I met him before?"

"Um . . . he might go to HMU. But don't worry, he's really, *really* nice and Luke sort of introduced him to me."

"Oh gosh, a college boy. I don't know how I feel about that."

"I'll be in college soon, too, you know."

"At least with your sister I always knew everything up front. Boys would barely say two words to her without asking permission."

"I'm not Greenie, Mom," I say, shifting my bag to my left shoulder.

"I'm very aware of that."

"We're just meeting for coffee."

"For the first time? Or is this what you've been doing after school every day? Have you been seeing a boyfriend secretly?" Her voice hushes and she sounds excited about this possibility rather than angry that I might be hiding something from her. Which I'm not. Not really.

"It's the first time we're going out, Mom. Sorry to disappoint."

"Can you at least tell me his name?"

"Jamie," I answer, and glance at the clock.

"I can't help being curious, Olivia. I'm a mother and mothers want to know things. It's our job."

"It's coffee, not marriage."

"Well, I've been a little concerned about you lately, to be honest, honey. You're never home. Where have you been then, if not with a boyfriend?—and don't tell me with Ash and Jada because they haven't been over here in ages."

"Oh. You know. Working hard on my story revisions. Father Mark is quite the taskmaster," I add.

"You've been with Father Mark?" She sounds genuinely surprised. "All these afternoons?"

I nod.

"He's being very generous with his time. You must have really impressed him with your writing, Olivia."

This time, I shrug. "Can I go now, please? I'll tell you more about Jamie later if I have anything significant to share. And if I don't leave soon I'm going to be late."

"Okay, go. Go." She moves aside and opens the door. "Have fun," she calls out as I run down the steps.

"Bye," I yell, turning down the sidewalk. I haven't even walked a block when my cell pings with a new text and I think, *Oh no, it's Jamie canceling, please don't let it be Jamie telling me he can't make it.* I take a deep breath, sit down on the bottom step of a neighbor's front stoop, and dig the cell from my bag, closing my eyes, preparing myself for the worst, and then look at the message that's popped up on the screen.

"Oh," I say out loud, when I see who it's from, my brow furrowing.

I can't believe I forgot that today was your last day of school, Olivia! Why don't we celebrate by going back to Eastern Standard? I'll see you at 7.

It's Father Mark.

I sit there, rereading the message and thinking for a long time, stuck in a loop of confusion about Father Mark's strange behavior earlier in his office, how he said he'd see me on the first day of class which isn't for two weeks, wondering whether he changed his mind or maybe he was just kidding, or he was even trying to punish me for knowing Jamie or something. But then, why would he do that? And now *this*, this invitation to see him barely two hours after his declaration about *not* seeing each other.

Is he just playing around? Testing me?

A faint pulse of anger travels through my veins.

Can't. Got plans, I punch in and hit Send. Then I turn the ringer to silent.

Tonight is about Jamie.

The mere thought of him acts like an instant pep talk, and one that gets me back up off the stoop and heading on my way, quickly now or I'll be late. *Jamie, Jamie,* I think in step with the click of my heels against the sidewalk, a steady, Jamie rhythm that eventually gives way to a growing excitement as I get closer to my destination, to our maybe-date, a feeling of anticipation that pushes aside the uncomfortable, awkward, painful moments of today. At least for now.

ON COLLEGE BOYS

BLINK. I CAN'T BELIEVE MY EYES. *BLINK*. JAMIE IS SITTING next to me, close enough to touch. Like it's no big deal. Like we hang out together all the time. One iced, low-fat vanilla latte, half-gone, sits in a giant plastic cup with a straw next to me and one cappuccino extra-shot, no sugar, with a few sips left next to him. I fight the urge to pinch myself. Jamie's left arm rests on the table barely an inch from mine, a wide leather cuff around his wrist. Electricity darts back and forth between us. I imagine I see sparks. Little lightning bolts. If I move my pinky just a tiny bit—

"Your turn," he says to me, and rests his hand along the side of his beautiful face.

"What's your major?" We are playing a little game of back and forth. He asks me something then I ask him.

"Philosophy," he answers. "I declared it this spring. I decided to do a lot of brooding during my college years."

"You don't seem like someone who wallows," I observe. Feel my heart race.

"Yeah, well, you've only been hanging around me for . . . let's see . . ." He looks up at the clock on the wall. "A little over two hours."

"True. So do you have a favorite philosopher yet?" I ask, even though I've read very little philosophy—mainly novels when I think about it, like *The Stranger* by Albert Camus.

"Nietzsche," he answers without hesitation.

"Huh. Really?"

"You sound surprised."

"I didn't take you for a 'God is dead' kind of guy." I wish I was daring enough to reach out and catch the tiny silver cross dangling from his neck between my fingers.

"Nietzsche is more complicated on the subject than people give him credit," Jamie explains. "But that's a longer conversation for another day."

So there'll be another day?

"My turn," he says.

"Ask your question."

"So are you excited about the class?"

The class.

My honest answer at the moment: yes and no. Today at least, I feel conflicted. What I say to Jamie: "Yes, I've been looking forward to it since the day I found out I had a spot."

"Me, too," he says. "It's almost eight p.m., which means I've been excited for just over three whole hours. And now I'm wondering whether you'll pretend you don't know me the first day—perhaps not a bad idea." He gives me a look, and I know Jamie is thinking about Father Mark's strange behavior earlier in his office. "Or: are you going to lower yourself and sit with the likes of me?" Now he is flirting.

"I might consider it." My hand shifts. Closer to his. "If you continue to be nice and entertaining." Almost there. Hands almost touching.

"Oh, I can be entertaining," Jamie says as if it's a challenge. His face lights up like there is more to say on the subject.

"Really? Do tell," I press, because I want to know everything about him, especially those things that make him come alive.

"I was going to wait until later to bring this up, but since we're on the subject . . ." He breathes in deep, readying himself for whatever comes next. "So my friends and I sometimes do this thing."

"Um, that's vague. You and your friends do a thing?"

"Give me a minute here. I'm working up to it." He smiles. Laughs. His eyes dart away and back.

"Okay. Sorry. I can be patient," I say, and think about how adorable Jamie is when he's nervous. "So what *kind* of thing?"

"It's really better if you see for yourself. The next gig is on Sunday afternoon—"

"Gig?"

"Yes, gig."

"So you're in a band?" Oh no. He's in a worship band and he's going to invite me to see him play bass for God like one of Greenie's friends.

"No, not a band." He rolls his eyes. "Don't worry, I'm not in one of those cheesy worship groups."

He read my mind. "I'll stop interrupting now."

"You sure? Got it all out?" He leans forward. Our faces are only inches apart. His arm moves closer to mine on the table.

"Positive," I say, determined not to move a muscle.

"So our next one is at St. John's parish this Sunday. It's for a bunch of youth groups—if you're not already busy, of course. There'll be food. There's a mass afterward. I thought maybe we could go together, to the mass I mean. Unless that makes you feel uncomfortable. I'd walk you home afterward."

Wow. Jamie asks me out on what sounds like a real date and it's to go to church. Greenie's going to love this, since it's basically her favorite kind.

"Sure, I'll go. I'd love to go. Sunday. Got it," I say, because I *would* love to go and because I'm curious what exactly "gig" means in this context. "You won't tell me what you're doing, though? For real?"

"Just promise you'll come. It'll be fun. I hope." He smiles. He's nervous again. "One o'clock."

"I'll be there."

"It's a date then." He places his hand on my arm for emphasis but all he emphasizes is the crackle of the current between us and the fact that we are finally touching, skin on skin, and I want to faint. "You better be careful, Olivia," he warns.

"Careful of what?" I am grinning, busy enjoying his nearness.

"Now you've made me two promises." His hand stays put and I find it difficult not to add mine to his.

"Two?"

"Sunday . . ."

"Yup. I remember that one." I ready myself to make a move, to take his hand.

"And the second is sitting with me in class every session—"

"Now we're up to every session? I don't know if I can commit that far," I kid, thinking, *Yes, yes, yes, absolutely, I will sit with you all summer if you want.*

"—*even* if you have to brave the wrath of your protective benefactor who has marked out special *Olivia Peters Only* reserved seating next to him up on the stage." Jamie laughs.

I don't.

Everything comes to a screeching halt with his suggestion, my mind, my body, my ability to speak, as if the Band-Aid was ripped off my wound too soon. Even though I know he isn't serious, all I can think is, *I don't want Jamie to act like I am a teacher's pet*, and then wonder, *But I am one, aren't I, though?* Finally, I respond. "That's ridiculous. Why would you even say that?"

"Because after seeing him with you this afternoon, I wouldn't be surprised."

I shift in my seat. Turn away. Stare at the people next to us.

"Hey, I was joking," he says.

"I know," I say, but I'm trying to imagine what Jamie saw in Father Mark's office that would make him think I'd be set apart from everyone else, if maybe my presence in Father Mark's office was somehow so out of the ordinary to someone who just happened upon us. I almost muster the nerve to ask him about this, straight-out, when he says, "Do you know how many students would kill to be in your shoes? If only I was as exceptionally talented as Olivia Peters." He is playing, trying to lighten up the conversation, but for some reason it only keeps upsetting me. Maybe it's because I'm worried I somehow did permanent damage to my situation with Father Mark and I'm still smarting from it. I can't decide.

My hands slide into my lap and we no longer touch. It's as if I've pulled some kind of plug and the electricity shuts off. "Let's talk about something else."

"I'm sorry. I meant to give you a compliment and instead I made you feel awkward." He looks pained.

"It's okay. Next question," I prompt, trying to get back to our game of back and forth. I'm not sure whose turn it is anymore but I decide to go next and go for broke as far as changing the subject because I want to take our topic as far away from Father Mark as possible, do some triage. I close my eyes, ready myself, then just blurt: "So, how many girlfriends have you had?"

His eyes widen and I detect a slight flush in his cheeks. This brings a small smile back to my face. My hands creep back onto the table until both my forearms rest there, in front of me.

"I plead the fifth on this one," he says. "Besides, there are plenty of other things you don't know about me yet."

"But I asked you about this in particular. The rules are, you have to answer."

"I didn't know there were rules."

"I might be making them up as we go." I am feeling better now. Ready to return to our conversation and the feelings of before.

"I see," he says, still avoiding the question.

"Answer, please: number of past girlfriends." It is my turn to act flirtatious now.

"You might never want to hang out with me again if I tell you."

"Why? Are there like, dozens? Hundreds?"

"No."

"Thousands?" I gasp in mock horror.

"No." He stares at his coffee mug instead of me.

"Then how bad can it be?"

"It's not that it's bad so much as it's . . . rather nonexistent." His eyes blink up from the mug, his lashes long, fluttering. Embarrassed.

"Tell me."

"Let's just say that I think I'm working on girlfriend number one as we speak." Jamie leans toward me. His hand slides along my forearm, slow, until it reaches my fingers.

"Oh," I whisper, my heart pounding in my chest.

"Hey . . . so . . . it's getting late and I should go. Can I walk you home?"

"Sure," I say, "yes."

"Excellent." We lock eyes, his confidence returning. Even when he gets up from his chair, he holds my gaze. "Shall we?"

I nod.

Without another word, we gather our things, and he buses the table. As we walk out of the coffee shop and down Newbury Street my left arm swings near his right. Occasionally our arms brush, sending invisible sparks into the atmosphere. Silence hangs between us except for the *swish, swish* of my dress, and everything is perfect, absolutely glorious, until the moment I check my cell to find out the time, but what I find instead, what I find in addition to the time, is that I have four missed calls and about ten new text messages all from the same person, and I can't help but think, *What has gotten into Father Mark today?*

The snapping shut of my phone is loud like a door slamming, which feels satisfying because I don't want to let anything else in right now, I want to shut everything else out, *I want to shut Father Mark out* because he does not belong here, between Jamie and me on our maybe-date. Besides, Father Mark is the one who said he'd see me the first day of class, and even if he lied—because he was obviously lying—I think maybe he had a point, that a break would be nice for all involved, and I'm going to hold him to that little stunt he pulled because two can play at that game even though I don't like being played with this way. I don't like it at all.

"Olivia?" Jamie inquires, pulling me out of my thoughts.

"Still here," I say, looking up, focusing on his big brown eyes, which are looking into mine.

"Good," he says.

That is all I need to forget: one word, one glance, one stare from Jamie as we walk—almost hand in hand, not quite, but almost—toward my house. With every step I find that my joy gets bigger and those nagging, unsettling feelings get further and further away until they have almost entirely disappeared from notice. But not quite.

ON URGENCY

FOR THE REMAINDER OF THE WEEK I TALK TO EVERYONE, all the time, everyone being Ash, Jada, Greenie, Luke, Mom, and Jamie, too—who has me counting the minutes until I see him again on Sunday.

Father Mark and I, on the other hand, do not talk at all, not since the day in his office, but not for lack of trying on his part. He's even started leaving little packages on the doorstep. I avoid his calls and texts and letters and gifts, dodging everything like a dodgeball champion on the playground. I don't know what possesses me to do this, to ignore him, to hold him to his word, as if performing a strange experiment. To see what happens if I simply don't pick up my cell, if I don't respond to any of his attempts to communicate, if I leave the letters that have begun arriving in the mailbox at our house unopened, notes that just last week I would have been eager to read the second they were in my hands. Now I just toss them onto the pile between the couch and the windowsill in my room. Ever since that day when I said, *No I can't meet you at Eastern Standard*, I've wondered what would happen if I continued

saying *no, no, no* to everything, instead of the usual *yes, yes, yes.*
I've wanted to know if Father Mark would eventually forget
about me.

And I find out. I learn something. His attention doesn't abate.
It increases.

It's not that I don't feel guilt—I do. I feel tremendous guilt
and like I am intentionally hurting this person who only wants
the best for me. But the moment I begin to avoid him the avoidance becomes something like an addiction because it brings me
relief. In all honesty I feel tremendous relief though I am not
sure why.

I thought I'd feel regret.

On Friday evening, when I open my laptop and log on to my
account, hoping to find Jamie online but finding instead e-mails
piling up in my mailbox, spaced only a few minutes apart, I'm
prompted to think—and not for the first time—*What has gotten
into him?* and *How can I calm him down?* I take the path of least
resistance and decide to open one and write a quick response.

Dear Olivia,

His e-mail begins.

Is everything all right? Are you okay? Is there something I did to upset you? If there is I apologize. I can't
help but worry. Please be in touch, just to let me
know if you are okay. And then, there's a special
event I want to talk to you about attending as my

guest. I need an answer soon, though. Please call or e-mail or text. I am waiting.

As always, he signs it,

Yours,
Mark

I write a short message back—*Dear Father Mark, Everything is fine! Just busy. See you in class week after next. Sincerely, Olivia Peters*—hit Send, and sigh. I have done my duty and now I can move on.

After waiting around online for a while, hoping to see Jamie, I am about to shut down when an instant message pops up on my screen:

MDBrendan: Olivia? Is that you? It's me. Mark.

I freeze. This is the first time Father Mark finds me this way and I know what I need to do: I have to answer. I have to. He can see me. He knows I am here. I have to explain to him. I owe him an explanation even though it feels like it might take all the energy in my body, but there is still something of the obedient Olivia in me and so I take a deep breath and begin to type.

Livvee17: Hey Father! What a surprise! You IM. Wow.
MDBrendan: Where have you been? I've been worried about why you aren't answering my calls or returning e-mails.
Livvee17: Yeah, about that. I'm really, really sorry. I just have a lot going on and you know, I need to

make time for my sister and my friends. They kind of get mad if I don't hang out with them. You know how it is, high school stuff. ☺

MDBrendan: Olivia, your number one priority needs to be your writing. I told you it can get lonely but that's what I am here for. I'm willing to do whatever it takes.

I'm in the middle of typing a response—But I didn't mean to—when another line from Father Mark pops up.

MDBrendan: End of discussion.

I don't know what to say to that. I can barely manage to type in But when Father Mark writes something else.

MDBrendan: Something has come up since we last spoke. There is an event we must go to and I need to RSVP. The people attending are important so it's crucial that you go. It's the James McDaniel book release party.

Livvee17: Wow! James McDaniel? Wow.

I am impressed, tempted by the offer, too tempted to say no, and this is when I remember why it's exciting to be around Father Mark.

MDBrendan: See, Olivia? These are important opportunities.

Livvee17: I know.

MDBrendan: I take that as a yes, then? You'll go.

Livvee17: Yes. Definitely. I will. I wouldn't miss it. Thank you for thinking of me.
MDBrendan: Good, good. Wonderful news. I'll RSVP for the both of us then, and send you the info.
Livvee17: Okay.

I can't help but feel pleased with myself. I want to stay in Father Mark's good graces because of the doors he is opening on my behalf. Why in the world would I do anything to get in the way of that? Maybe I've been too harsh and acting immature about this whole *we're not speaking* thing because I didn't like the way it felt to be scolded by him. I begin to think that maybe I should call off my little experiment, this little game of me running away from him, when I receive another IM—

MDBrendan: The next order of business is that we need to meet ASAP.

—and as soon as I read the words on the screen I know that I don't want to see him, that I can't because I am booked anyway— plans with Greenie tomorrow, Jamie on Sunday, Ash and Jada all through next week, and hopefully even more plans with Jamie if things go well this weekend. I take a deep breath and type what I know are Father Mark's two least favorite words, words that I've found so difficult to say to him, that I know will make him unhappy, maybe even angry:

Livvee17: I can't.
MDBrendan: What do you mean, you can't?

Livvee17: I have plans every day and night until class starts. Maybe we could meet that afternoon, the first day of class, to work beforehand? How does that sound? A good compromise, right? ☺

MDBrendan: What is so important that you can't meet with me immediately?

The cursor blinks and I don't know what to type. So I take the cowardly route.

Livvee17: My mom is calling me I gotta go, BYE! ☺

I slam my laptop shut, breathing hard. I'm covered in sweat.

My cell phone lights up on the couch next to me. I'm careful not to touch it. I don't feel ready to hash this out right now. When the ringing stops I grab it, wanting to shut it down but it immediately lights up again in my hand, startling me. I'm afraid if I try shutting it down I'll accidentally answer instead so I bury it under a pile of dirty laundry where it continues to ring. I shut my bedroom door and lie down on the rug. It feels soft underneath me and I close my eyes. I am so tired all of a sudden. Worn out. Eventually the ringing stops. But soon the thought that there is something . . . something going on that's . . . I don't know. But then, maybe I'm wrong. Maybe it's just in my head. Maybe I'm overreacting.

Yes. I'm sure that's it. It's just me and my overactive imagination.

Convincing myself of this is what allows me to eventually drift off to sleep right there, on the floor of my room, without even a blanket. And I wake like this on Saturday, stretched out and exposed in the light of the morning sun.

ON BEING WATCHED

GREENIE AND I SPEND ALL DAY SHOPPING FOR WEDDING dresses and I have fun playing maid of honor which, in addition to holding up mirrors and oohing and aahing at how beautiful my sister looks in everything she tries on, also includes prying information from her about kissing Luke and making her blush when I ask whether she has any wedding night jitters. But then Greenie turns the tables on me even though this is not her intent and says, "By the way, Mom said Father Mark is really serious about you—"

"Serious? What do you mean, serious?" I interrupt, but something inside me clicks and I realize that serious *is* the right word for how Father Mark acts toward me, that he's serious about having a role in my life, that he's taken my winning this contest very seriously. Maybe a little too seriously.

"You are so lucky," Greenie responds. "You realize that, right?"

"Yes," I say, because it's true and I do know. I know this all too well. "It's not that big a deal—" I try to add, but immediately Greenie is shushing me, believing that I am trying to be modest.

"Just enjoy it," she advises, and I can't help but think that *enjoy* is no longer the right word to describe this attention from Father Mark, but I am not quite sure when *enjoyable* turned into something more akin to *obligation* that might even be approaching *desperation* on his end these last few days. When we leave the bridal store and Greenie leads me down the street and into a chocolate shop I am reminded of the first time Father Mark and I got together and the pathetic, powdery hot chocolate I tried to force down because I'd ordered it and didn't want to be rude and how silly and childish I felt. The memory sends an unpleasant shiver up my spine, my body prickling, and I can't help thinking, *So much has changed since then.*

But then Greenie shifts the subject to Jamie. She wants to know all about our coffee date and how he walked me home and how I am going to church with him tomorrow—*How romantic,* she says. This pulls me out of my funk, my weird Father Mark funk, and I roll my eyes at my sister and remind her, "Greenie, I'm not you," because we may both be Catholic but I am not in the same league as she and Luke on that front. "Though I know you mean well," I add, because I don't want to hurt her feelings, but then it's Greenie's turn to roll her eyes and inform me that she is not as sensitive as she looks. This prompts a shift to a good maid of honor topic, which is her bridal shower, and I tell her that if she's not careful I'm going to tell her friends to bring only lingerie as gifts.

When Greenie turns bright red I can't keep from laughing, and soon she is laughing, too, and we continue like this, talking for hours, catching up, trading stories, until Greenie is hugging me goodbye and heading off to see Luke for dinner and I am rushing to meet Ash and Jada down the street at Jada's favorite new yogurt place before we go to the movies tonight.

As I walk down Newbury a tiny voice from somewhere deep tells me how much I enjoy all this Father Mark–free time—which hasn't technically been Father Mark–free, but I've made it so. And when my cell lights up with Father Mark's number on the caller ID, it feels right not to answer it, and when it lights up again not even a minute later, I just forward the call to voice mail and determine not to give it another thought because *he* started this—*he said it*, I didn't—*I'll see you in class, Olivia*, and I assumed he meant it. Regardless of his real intentions—whatever they were, *are*—I am taking a Father Mark vacation, one that belongs to me, the old Olivia, before I won the contest.

But then later on when Ash and Jada and I are walking to the movie theater, each of us sipping our yogurt smoothies and Jada has caught us up on all things Sam and I am gushing about Jamie, and Ash bets that after our date tomorrow Jamie will begin following me around like a lovesick puppy, Jada says something next that stops me cold.

"You have priests following you so it wouldn't surprise me if Jamie was next." She is only half kidding.

"What do you mean?" Something in Jada's voice, something leads me to wonder.

"You mean you didn't see him?"

"See who?" I ask, but I think I know, I think I already know.

"Father Mark," she says, and seems genuinely surprised.

"What are you talking about?" I ask, and think, *Please let her be wrong.*

"He walked by the yogurt place, like, four times while we were in there."

"He did?"

"I think it was him."

"Oh," I say, feeling a little dizzy. "If it really was him, he was probably on his way to HMU. He always walks down Newbury Street."

"On a Saturday night?"

"Um . . . maybe it was just someone who looked like him," I say, because what else is there to say? I glance around, behind me, to my left, right, looking, searching because I can't help it, and once I am sure the coast is clear, Father Mark–clear, I change the subject back to Sam which Jada happily picks back up as if we'd never left the topic. No matter how hard I try to focus, I am left thinking that something is off, that Father Mark and I just need to figure out how to strike a better balance, and when things calm down—when *he* calms down—we will talk about this and everything will turn out all right. I am sure he will understand. He will. He has to.

ON ROMANCE

SUNDAY AFTERNOON FINALLY ARRIVES AND I AM LAUGH-
ing hard, doubled over, tears pouring down my face. My hands
grip the armrests of the chair as I try to pull myself together so I
can see because I don't want to miss a moment. Jamie and his
friends, their Sunday "gig" at St. John's, turns out to be Catholic
improv—which, I know, sounds totally lame, but it's so *not*. The
auditorium in the church hall is packed, standing room only, and
I was lucky to get a seat in the back. If I wasn't in love with Jamie
already I am now, because he is so unbelievably, amazingly funny,
and I am fairly sure that the several hundred other screaming girls
in the room agree.

They call themselves the Holy Fools.

In the span of an hour they have made fun of everything ridiculous about growing up Catholic—catechism classes, Catholic
school uniforms, nuns and priests, the Pope and his funny hat,
ridiculous saint deaths, being forced to go to mass as a kid, the
many uses of those palms they give you on Palm Sunday. Somehow they do all of this without being offensive. Pure Catholic
comedy. Who would've thought?

"Your favorite childhood Bible stories, people. What are they?" The only girl among the four asks the audience to name some examples, and she follows this with another request, this time for types of music. Opera, country, Irish drinking songs, *American Idol*–style, yodeling, and Broadway musical are among the suggestions, and soon she steps up to the mike and sings, "The Virgin Birth!" in a ridiculous falsetto. Before the skit is over, the group performs "Adam and Eve" the musical, "The Prodigal Son" *American Idol*–style, complete with a lot of off-key belting, and "Samson and Delilah" like an Irish drinking song. After the last lines of "Job" are yodeled, Jamie goes up to the mike and says, "Thank you very much," and quiets everyone down for what I expect to be a solemn prayer to conclude the afternoon, but what turns out to be a funny montage of the Nicene Creed, the Our Father, and the prayer of penitence, and everyone is laughing again.

Afterward, as people file out the back and into the church for mass, I head toward the front of the auditorium so I can find Jamie and learn that I'm not the only one hanging around. About a hundred girls crowd the stage and I hear them talking about "how totally dreamy" the one with the dark hair and eyes is— that's Jamie—and I can't help smiling and thinking to myself, *I am with him, yes, the dreamy one.*

I hover at the back of the crowd, moving forward as it begins to thin out, and Jamie smiles back at me. He makes his way over, signing a T-shirt for a fan in between.

"There you are." He seems surprised to see me.

"Of course. I promised I'd be here."

"I was looking for you before we started and couldn't find

you in the audience. I thought maybe you flaked. Or decided it was too uncool to meet up with a guy at church."

"I was way in the back," I explain. "But I saw everything and it was a-*may*-zing."

"Thanks." His smile grows. God, he's beautiful. "You're kind."

"No, I'm serious. I haven't laughed that hard in ages. You guys are like Catholic *SNL* or something."

"Really?" He thinks I'm just being nice.

"Honest." A girl walks up, asking Jamie to sign another T-shirt, and I remember we are not alone. I'd almost forgotten there are people milling around us. He finishes, hands her Sharpie back, and she takes off, somewhat reluctantly, I notice. "Definitely not a worship band."

"No way. Besides, I didn't get the musical talent gene, in case you couldn't tell from the singing during the show."

"But that's what made it so funny."

"Anything for laughs."

"Do you do this for fun, or is it, like, a job?"

"The Holy Fools is paying my way through college."

"Really? That's great. Beyond great." Jamie is smart, nice, hot, *and* impressive.

"Hey, so I wanted to introduce you to everyone. Is that cool?" He glances around, back at their merchandise table. The rest of the group is packing T-shirts and other paraphernalia into gigantic black duffel bags.

"Sure." I can't help becoming a little nervous as he leads me toward the stage and everyone stops what they are doing, as if already prepped for an introduction.

"Hi, Olivia," one of them says, all friendly, and I think, *He already knows my name!* "I'm Nathan. Great to have you here. Break it to us gently—what'd you think?"

"You were incredible. I loved it."

"Well, aren't you sweet."

"I'm Hailey." The only girl in the group walks up and extends her hand to shake mine. "Jamie told us you were coming today. It's great to meet you."

"Yeah, he wouldn't shut up about it, either," says a short, stocky guy with a bowl haircut. Jamie punches him in the arm, which I assume means that the friend should keep his mouth shut on the me-issue. "I'm Jonas. A pleasure."

"Don't worry, Jamie said only nice things," Hailey whispers, leaning in so no one else hears. "You are one lucky girl, you know." We both turn to look at Jamie, who has gone over to help the others finish breaking down the display.

"I am in total agreement with that statement."

Hailey smiles. "He hasn't stopped talking about you since the day you met."

"Really?"

She nods.

"Come on, Hailey. Time to go." Jonas brushes by me, heading up the aisle carrying two merchandise bags, one over each shoulder, barely able to walk. Hailey smiles and walks over to the table, hoisting one of the bags over her shoulder and following Jonas toward the door. As Nathan passes me on his way out he asks, "You're coming to church, right?" When I answer, "Yes," he calls back, "Now don't you two get all caught up in each other or you'll be late."

Jamie rolls his eyes. "Sorry about that. They're just . . . *excited*."

"Excited?"

"Yeah . . . well . . . yeah."

"How so?"

"Because I invited you."

"You don't usually have guests attend shows?"

"We have guests. Just not special guests."

"Special?" My insides jump up and down with glee.

"You're the first girl I've ever had come to one of these and, you know, to church afterward. They're sort of in shock."

"You don't invite girls every week?" I already know the answer but I want to hear him say it.

"The honor is yours only." He looks around and under the merchandise table making sure nothing is left behind, maybe using this as an excuse to look away. Definitely blushing. Jamie is blushing. "I think they took everything. So . . . do you want to go?"

"To church?"

"Yes. But don't feel pressured. I have to attend mass, though. I always go after we perform. It's kind of part of the gig."

"I'm going. I want to."

"Good." He relaxes again, offering his hand, a gesture for us to head up the aisle. He weaves his fingers through mine and we leave the auditorium and enter the packed church. Nathan, Hailey, and Jonas have saved us room in the pew. As soon as we slide in next to them, the priest starts the procession and everyone stands.

After the opening prayers, we sit again as the deacon goes through the first reading. Little by little, Jamie's fingers creep closer to mine, until our pinkies touch, then wrap around each other, and soon one, two, three, all our fingers are entwined. We stay like this, touching fingers, brushing palms, pulling apart for different prayers and rituals, only for our hands to find each other again, all the while staring at the altar, at the priest. The mass happens around us for the next hour. My heart speeds up, slows down, leaps, and speeds up again, thumping in my chest, and for once I wish with all my being that the priest would not come to those closing words, *Our mass has ended, let us go in peace.* I hadn't known going to church could be so romantic. If it was always like this I'd go to daily mass.

As Jamie and I file out behind the crowd, I notice someone out of the corner of my eye, a man standing there, looking at me, at *us.*

A Father Mark–looking man.

My head snaps right but no one is there and I think, *God, Olivia, now you are seeing things.* Jamie turns to me, his eyes searching, inquiring, and I smile in response, concentrate on his hand in mine, steadying myself and determining to be in this moment, the here and now, because the here and now is about as good as things get and my time with Jamie isn't even over yet. We have the entire afternoon ahead of us and today is about Jamie only and nothing, nobody, can do anything to change this. Not even Father Mark. If that's who I saw. Which I didn't. Because it wasn't. Him.

ON POETRY

THE NEXT WEEK FLIES BY AND BEFORE I KNOW IT I AM getting ready to head out for the first meeting of Father Mark's fiction class. I am a jumble of nerves and confusion. The strange dance of avoidance between Father Mark and me has intensified and we still haven't seen each other since that day in his office, which seems like a long time ago now. Well, I haven't seen him at least. But Jamie and I, on the other hand, have gotten together daily since the Sunday of our church date, and he is even walking me to class and home afterward and I am more excited about this than class itself. It's difficult to ignore how my feelings about Father Mark and the class and even the contest have changed—it wasn't long ago that I was counting the days because I couldn't wait for the seminar to begin.

Mom and I stand around in the kitchen, drinking lemonade, waiting for Jamie to arrive—she insists on meeting him this time—when the doorbell rings. I run to answer it, but Mom gets there first.

"Hello, Jamie. Come on in. It's nice to finally meet you." She steps aside. Mom is all smiles.

"Hi, Ms. Peters. Nice to meet you, too." Jamie flashes me a grin on his way into the foyer.

"We should get going so we aren't late," I say, hoping for a quick getaway.

"No, no," Mom protests, looking up at the clock, which says three, giving us a full hour before class begins. "Please, sit down." She ushers Jamie into the living room. "Can I get you anything to drink?"

"Just water if you don't mind, thanks."

"We have lemonade."

"Lemonade would be great then."

"Olivia, what about you? Would you like more?"

"Fine, fine," I give in, handing her my half-empty glass.

Mom returns with the drinks, sits down on the couch, and the questions begin.

"Where are you from originally, Jamie?"

Cape Cod. Born and raised by the beach.

"How do you like HMU so far?"

A lot. Great professors. Great classes. Great city.

"I hear you're quite the comedian."

The conversation continues like this for what seems like forever. Jamie is at ease, as if he meets people's parents all the time, and Mom is having fun grilling him. It appears I am the only anxious person in the room. I guzzle my lemonade and then sit there, fidgeting, while Jamie continues to answer Mom's inquiries with enthusiasm, even making a few of his own, until finally, I cut in. "Mom, it's three-forty."

She glances at the clock. "All right, Olivia. You win. Besides, I wouldn't want to be the reason you two are late for Father

Mark!" She sings his name. "Especially when he's coming for dinner later this week."

"He is?" I am startled.

"He is!" She is exuberant.

"But when—"

"He called the house and we made a plan. You know I've been wanting to celebrate your win. I'm so proud of her," she says to Jamie, beaming.

"He called the house?"

"I know it's difficult for you to remember, but we still have a landline, Olivia. He said he was having trouble getting in touch with you on your cell—I didn't get you a cell for you to ignore it, by the way." She gives me a scolding look. "Anyway, he and I got to talking and I invited him over for a dinner in your honor."

"That's great," I say, my heart sinking a little as Jamie and I stand up, getting ready to head out. The end of my Father Mark vacation has officially arrived. I need to work on remembering how time with Father Mark used to be so exciting and not so—I don't know, dread-inducing? But I'm confident this feeling has more to do with nerves that will dissipate as soon as we do see each other again and things go back to the way they were before.

"Ready?" Jamie asks after the requisite "Nice to meet you's" and "Thanks for the lemonade" from him to my mom, and I say, "Yes," and launch myself through the foyer, out the door, and down the steps while Jamie is still exchanging pleasantries with my mother. When he finally makes his way over to where I am waiting not so patiently, he is chuckling.

"What," I demand. "What?"

"You are cute when you get nervous." He stops in front

of me, close enough to kiss, but then he holds out his hand instead, reaching for mine. "We should walk fast," he says. "It's almost four."

"How 'bout I race you instead," I challenge, taking off before he can answer. Even though it is warm out and my bag bounces against my side it feels good to run, to release some of the excess energy I feel, and by the time we reach the campus gates I am laughing and both of us are trying to catch our breath. Jamie lies down in the grass on the quad, his chest rising and falling, and I join him, so we are side by side, and he turns to me. "I let you beat me."

"That is such a guy thing to say."

"Well, I'm a guy."

Despite my exhaustion, I can't let his comment slide so I heave myself off the ground, again taking off, this time toward Gregory Hall, shouting, "I bet you can't catch me even if you try your hardest." Jamie is up and running after me and in less than a minute we are both across the courtyard and at the entrance to the building, tagging the wall. Neither of us can tell who got here first so we call a truce. It must be late because we are alone.

"So after class, I thought we could go to the Public Garden," Jamie says, in between breaths, before we go inside.

"Okay," I agree, deciding that I will show him my favorite place, the bench under the willow tree, thinking that this is a nice idea—to share a place so special to me with Jamie.

"We should really go in. It's after four."

"Oh. Yeah. Sure." I am hesitant, reluctant even, but I follow Jamie inside, consoling myself that we have three hours of sharing an armrest and being near each other ahead of us. When we reach the auditorium he opens the door to let me go first. Father Mark's voice carries into the hallway and I tiptoe inside, trying to be quiet. Jamie follows and we grab two spots in the back row. *Creak* go the theater-style seats when we push them down. *Creak.* Father Mark stops speaking and peers from the podium into the audience packed with students, staring at the latecomers, zeroing in on us. On me. Entering his classroom late. Disrespectful. He stops long enough that I wonder what he is thinking, if he is upset. His reading glasses fall from his face and dangle on their chain. Papers rustle. He picks up his eyeglasses without moving his gaze from mine and I suddenly feel prickly. Hot. Cold. Uncomfortable. Guilty.

Then he returns to what he was saying and I sigh with relief.

Looking up at him now, standing there on the stage, so tall and confident, it seems strange to have witnessed this same person become frantic and unnerved. For a passing moment I feel ashamed about my recent behavior, my resistance, the rebellious daughter testing the boundaries and the patience of the father.

After going over the syllabus, expectations for attendance, and assignments, to which I only half listen because my other half is otherwise occupied with Jamie's proximity, Father Mark explains that he will end tonight's class early, that he'll see us again next week—and to make sure we check our assignment—but that before we go he'll read a poem aloud, that he'll do this at every class meeting. When he announces his selection—Pablo Neruda's "Sonnet XVII" to be read in both English and the original Spanish—he regains my full attention. My cheeks catch fire because I immediately know what he means to do.

"Olivia Peters, please join me on the stage," he says in that booming voice of his, now amplified even bigger by the sound system.

I sink down further in my chair and it groans from the move-ment. Jamie leans toward me and whispers, "You'll do great."

"Don't be shy, Olivia," Father Mark says into the mike.

Feeling dazed, I get up from my seat—*creak*—and make my way to the front of the auditorium, up the stairs and onto the stage. All the while Father Mark is explaining how I am a special student in this class because I won a contest, *his* contest, that I show great promise and he is thrilled to have me here. He's decided to introduce me to everyone through the Nobel Prize–winning poet Pablo Neruda, because he knows that Neruda is one of my favorites. I climb the stairs to the stage, listening to his words, how he describes me to everyone as if we are on the best of terms, as if I hadn't just walked in late to our first class meeting and avoided him entirely these last couple of weeks.

When I arrive at the podium my heart is pounding and my hands are shaking, but Father Mark is smiling, like he is loving this, loving not only standing up in front of everyone, but stand-ing up in front of everyone with me. He shifts sideways, barely, and points to the papers on the lectern. On the left is a copy of the Neruda poem in Spanish, and on the right, a copy of it trans-lated into English.

I hesitate.

"If you had come to my office this afternoon like you prom-ised weeks ago you would have been prepared," Father Mark whis-pers in my ear, sending a shiver through me but not the good kind, and immediately I want this over with so I begin.

"Hello," I say, and remind myself to breathe, squeezing even closer to Father Mark so I can speak into the mike. "Pablo Neruda's *Soneto Diecisiete*," I begin to read, slowly, deliberately, trying to pronounce everything correctly. As I process the meaning of Neruda's words I think, *What an odd choice Father Mark has made,* but this passes quickly and soon I am done, the class applauds, and it is Father Mark's turn to read the English. I am about to walk away when Father Mark hands me the sheet with the poem on it and says, "This is for you, Olivia," and I smile and take it because what else can I do? We are on the stage in front of an auditorium filled with his student admirers. Before Father Mark can utter the first line I am across the stage and heading down the steps, the paper crinkling in my sweaty hands, listening as he reads.

I do not love you as if you were salt-rose, or topaz,
or the arrow of carnations the fire shoots off.
I love you as certain dark things are to be loved,
in secret, between the shadow and the soul.

As I make my way back to my seat I tune out the rest, only catching one more line—*so I love you because I know no other way*—before I am sitting again next to Jamie who smiles at me like everything is wonderful and I did a good job. When my fingers grip the armrest he places his hand on mine and I begin to relax again, remembering that soon I will be heading off with him to the Public Garden for a romantic evening. But sneaking into my thoughts are questions like *Has Father Mark always been this strange? This awkward?* and *Did something change or did I just not notice it before?*

After finishing the last line of the poem, Father Mark dismisses us and we file out, slow, up the aisles and out of the auditorium into the warm summer evening. Students congregate in the courtyard, chatting, because it is the kind of weather that makes you want to linger, but Jamie and I don't because I want to leave right away.

"Let's go," I say, and take his hand, trying to pull him across the courtyard. Jamie lags behind, glancing at the students hanging out near Gregory Hall.

"No more races tonight, Olivia. Slow down."

And so I do because he is right and I am being silly with all this rushing.

"Don't you want to see what other people thought of our first class? Of all the fuss he made out of you, Olivia?"

"Not really."

"You shouldn't be embarrassed. He's proud of you."

"Let's just go."

"I know that for you seeing Father Mark is normal, but it's new for me."

This comment halts me and I turn to face him. "I'm sorry. I should've thought . . . I should've been more sensitive . . . I just wasn't thinking. Do you want to go back?"

He steps closer and takes my other hand. Looks at me. Hesitates. Unsure what to do.

That's when I see Father Mark out of the corner of my eye. Watching us from afar. Suddenly I want to run. Panic flickers across my face.

"I guess we can hang out after class another night," Jamie says, finally, and thankfully I am soon tugging him again, walking so quickly across the quad that it prompts Jamie to remind me once more about how we are not running a race.

"So did you enjoy the class?" I ask, once we are safely through the campus gates, because I feel guilty, like I somehow cheated

Jamie out of the full Father Mark seminar experience, which included gushing afterward with our fellow classmates.

"I did. I don't care if he's assigned piles of work. The opportunity to take his class was one of my goals when I decided to attend HMU. He's just brilliant, you know?" Jamie looks straight at me, eyes locked, as we walk along the sidewalk, but I can't enjoy the moment. The mention of Father Mark's greatness sends a wave of nausea rolling through me. "He made such a big deal out of you tonight," Jamie presses, excited on my behalf.

"Nah. It was only a poem."

"Don't be so modest."

"I'm really looking forward to the rest of the class, of course." I'm doing my best to muster enthusiasm so I don't rain any more on Jamie's parade. "Public speaking makes me nervous, though. Unlike for some people I know." I give Jamie a playful shove, relieved to shift the topic even if only a small amount.

"Are you referring to my improv group? Is there something I actually do better than the talented Olivia Peters?" Jamie grins, swinging my hand in his as we turn onto Arlington Avenue, near the entrance to the Public Garden.

"Maybe." I return the grin as we enter the park and make our way down the path and around the beautiful flower beds. Soon I settle back into a happy place where there is only Jamie and me holding hands, walking along as if we have all the time in the world. I lead him toward my spot, the bench under the weeping willow tree, the same bench by the lake where "The Girl in the Garden" takes place, because I want to share it with him, this part of myself that has enough history to go all the way back to my dad, my real father, who took me here when I was small.

"Wow," he says, when we arrive and sit down, looking out over the water, close enough that our shoulders touch. "It's beautiful. I can't believe I've never been before."

"I'm glad you like it."

The sun drops little by little, until the rose red of the summer's evening tips into bright blue twilight just before dark. We talk for hours, about his family, why he became a philosophy major, his faith, how he never knew he was funny until he got to HMU, and how he's always been shy. He asks me questions, too, about growing up in Boston, about my writing, my favorite color, my favorite flavor of ice cream. I tell him about how Dad left when I was little and what it was like to grow up with priests substituting as fathers. How my mother is an amazing woman though she'd never say so herself. And I tell him about "The Girl in the Garden," how, in the story, a girl magically appears one day to a boy who visits this spot every afternoon and they fall in love. But I leave out the part about heartbreak because right now discussing heartbreak doesn't seem the right way to go. The only answers I do my best to keep short or avoid altogether are the ones to do with Father Mark, even though Jamie is eager to hear every last detail of what I know about the man and whether he's revealed anything special about how to succeed in class this summer. Eventually, after yet another one-word answer, Jamie changes the subject to something far more preferable.

Jamie asks whether I've ever dated anyone. Just one person, no one important, I tell him. There's never been anyone significant, not until recently. Not until him. And that's when we look into each other's eyes. We lean toward one another and kiss for the first time. Then we kiss once more. We are about to kiss again and I am elated and lost in the moment when something slides out of my bag and floats to the ground by our feet and Jamie turns to see what it is.

The paper with the Neruda poem sits alongside the lake's edge. Jamie reaches down to pick it up before the wind takes it sailing into the water, holds it up toward the lamplight overhead. "Huh," he says. "Did you notice that there is another poem on the back?"

"No." I resist the urge to snatch it from his hands to put it away. He reads aloud:

"For M. in October," by Thomas Merton

If we could come together like two parts
Of one love song
Two chords going hand in hand
A perfect arrangement
And be two parts of the same secret
(Oh if we could recover
And tell again
Our midsummer secret!)

If you and I could even start again as strangers
Here in this forsaken field
Where crickets rise up
Around my feet like spray
Out of a green ocean . . .
But I am alone,
Alone walking up and down
Leaning on the silly wind
And talking out loud like a madman

"If only you and I
Were possible."

Goose bumps stand up on my arms.

"Interesting choice," Jamie says. "Do you know Merton's history?"

I turn my head to look at him, force myself to admit, "No. I don't. What is it?"

"Merton was a Trappist monk, a famous one—famous for his writing, kind of like Father Mark actually. When he was in his fifties he got sick and was in the hospital for a long time. While he was there, he fell in love with his nurse."

"Really."

"She was only like, twenty-two or something."

"Oh." I am strangled into silence. *Oh,* I think, then quickly swat this unpleasant thought away.

"No kidding. Creepy."

"Yeah. Creepy."

Something inside me twists, contorts, but I can't let myself go *there* so instead I use all my energy to focus on Jamie and how I should enjoy my Jamie time while I have it. This determination plants itself firmly and so I let the poem, Father Mark, the class, the rest of the world, my sense of it, disappear until me and Jamie are all that is left, on the bench under the weeping willow tree, kissing. Kissing some more. And when at one point Jamie leans back to take a breath and in the silence those thoughts, the thoughts I want to erase, begin to push their way back into my mind, I lean forward and say to Jamie, "Kiss me again," and he does and I am saved.

ON CHARLES BEACH

SWISH, SWISH. MY FEET BRUSH THROUGH THE GRASS AS I make my way along the bank of the Charles River, flip-flops and sunglasses dangling from one hand, a stainless-steel travel mug filled with coffee grasped in the other. In my bag is a big blanket with the novel I'm reading and Father Mark's story edits, which I vow to deal with today. Once and for all. There is a nice breeze—there usually is at this time of the morning. The summer smell of green fills the air and the glare on the river is bright and glitters in the sun. I set up my stuff—coffee, book, a flip-flop holding down each corner of the blanket by my feet. The edits, though, I leave safely tucked away in my bag. For now.

Mom, Greenie, and I call this place Charles Beach. We've been having picnics here since I was a kid, though I don't know how it got its name. It's most definitely not a beach, especially since there's no sand and to get here you have to cross a bridge over Storrow Drive. Even this far down the bank near the water you can hear cars whizzing by in the background—and the Charles, though a big river, isn't the ocean. Not even close. Noise and all, I love it. The rhythmic lap of the water against the river's edge, the *pat, pat, pat* of the morning joggers passing behind me on the path, the rowers gliding across the water, so smooth, so fast, so silent, so together. Lying on the blanket in the grass with my novel and my coffee all to myself. This is my sacred time.

I put on my sunglasses and prop myself up on my elbows, watching the crew boats from Harvard, MIT, HMU. I enjoy the view and daydream about Jamie and sigh, relaxed.

Then, out of the corner of my eye I notice the manuscript edge that peeks out from the top of my bag and it chips away at my peace. I'm beginning to think Father Mark's demand for revisions will never end, that working on this story is no longer about making it publishable, but an excuse for him to be in constant touch with me.

And if I just could take away his excuse . . .

"I thought I'd find you here," says a voice from above, startling me for a second before I realize it's only my mother.

I take off my sunglasses and turn to see her looking down at me, her head blocking the sun, her short hair hanging forward in two slants that frame her chin. She holds a glass of orange juice in one hand and a large Tupperware container in the other.

"Did you just walk that glass of juice over the highway?"

"Well it didn't walk itself." She moves to sit down and I am practically blinded by the glare of the sun. "What a gorgeous day." She parks herself on my blanket, sitting cross-legged in her light blue seersucker Mom-shorts, culottes she calls them. "You left without eating *again* and I'm a mom so I worry about these things. You are getting so skinny, Olivia."

Her concern gets to me so I take the container she holds out. Ham, egg, and cheese on an English muffin. My favorite.

Immediately I feel a stab of guilt. Mom likes to call this particular breakfast Heart Attack on a Plate so she must be desperate to get me to eat. Even though I'm not really hungry I take a big bite and force it down. "That was really nice of you, to carry this all the way from the house and over Storrow Drive," I say, and smile, doing my best to ease her worry, wanting to give her the impression that everything is fine and dandy.

"I'm not leaving until you finish the entire sandwich."

"I'm not five anymore."

"Yes, but lately you've hardly touched your food."

"That's not true," I say, nibbling away, talking with my mouth full to try and make her scold me or at least laugh.

"You may not be five, but I can tell when one of my daughters is pushing things around on her plate to make it look like she's eaten."

I don't have a good response to this.

"Olivia?"

"Hmmm?"

"Is everything okay?"

"Yup. Perfect." I shove the rest of the sandwich in my mouth, gulping it down, hoping this will satisfy her.

"Let's talk about Father Mark," she proposes, and I almost spit everything back up. I wait to respond until I am sure that everything has been safely swallowed.

"What about him?" My words are slow. Hesitant.

"He's coming for dinner this week. Remember? And I don't know what to cook yet."

"He'll like whatever you make."

"But I want it to be special."

"We have priests over all the time," I say, as if this explains everything. "It's not as if Father Mark is any different."

"We have *Father MacKinley* over all the time. And Father Mark *is* different. You know that."

I wish everyone would stop acting like Father Mark is such a big deal. This is what I think but don't have the guts to say out loud.

"Olivia?"

"What? Sorry. I got distracted."

"I can see I'm getting nowhere."

"Hmmm" is the noncommittal sound that comes out of my mouth.

"Please think about what he might like." She signals a willingness to let the subject drop, and then, "Ooh, is that your story I see?"

"No," I lie, but Mom reaches over my leg and pulls it out of my bag. I grab it from her hands with such force that I hear her hiss in pain.

"Ow, you gave me a paper cut!"

"Mom, I'm sorry . . . I didn't mean to . . ." Tears spring into my eyes. I turn the manuscript facedown, out of her reach. I don't want her near anything having to do with Father Mark and what he writes to me because it is my problem and not hers and I don't want her to see. I just don't.

She takes one of the napkins she brought with breakfast and presses it over her finger, trying to stop the bleeding.

"Why won't you show me?" She sounds hurt.

"Um . . . because Father Mark made me promise not to let anyone see until it's finished. It's still a work in progress . . . you know how it is . . ." I bank on the fact that she will somehow understand what I mean because she is a writer.

"All right." She hesitates, then continues, "I suppose I can appreciate that. Especially if he asked this of you and you are trying to respect his wishes."

"If the circumstances were different you know I'd show you, right? Because I would."

Her smile reappears at this, and I know I've said the right thing, fixed everything. At least for now. "What an opportunity, Olivia." She sighs, made content by this thought. "How fun that you get to go through this process with Father Mark Brendan!" She beams with pride that I've somehow hit the writer-mentor jackpot. "If you don't want to talk about dinner or your story, maybe you can tell me how things are going with Jamie?" At the mention of Jamie, my face lights up and this encourages Mom to press on. "I liked him very much, Olivia, in the thirty minutes you allowed me to talk to him," she says.

"Thirty-five."

"Sorry. The thirty-*five* minutes."

"I like him, too, Mom."

"I can tell." She stretches her legs out and leans back against her arms, turning her face toward the sun. Getting comfortable. We sit there a long time like this, first talking about Jamie, then in quiet, the two of us staring out at the water.

My earlier anxiety has almost faded to nothing and then . . .

"What are you thinking?" Mom asks after our long silence.

"I don't know. Nothing really."

"Is there something wrong, sweetheart? You've been acting so strange, so quiet lately. You're usually so exuberant and full of life. It's like someone drained you or—"

"No," I practically shout, then lower my voice. "I'm fine. Really. Enjoying the day."

"Oh, Olivia."

"Everything is great. I swear."

"Are you sure?"

"Yes. Absolutely." I am firm. Definitive.

Mom's eyebrows raise, but she doesn't pry further. "Okay then. I've done my duty here. I've fed you. I've made you tell me about your new boyfriend or whatever you are calling him. I'll leave you to your morning." She gets up from the blanket, shading her eyes as she looks at me. "Can you hand me the glass and the container?"

"Sure," I say, and she takes them, balancing one on top of the other. "Thanks, Mom. For breakfast. It was really nice of you."

"You're welcome. I'm glad you ate."

"I'm glad you came down to visit. It's nice. Like old times." I pick up my novel and open it. "Okay . . . I'm going to read now."

"I get the hint."

"Mom," I call out as she heads up the bank toward the bridge, slow, steady, taking her time. "I love you!"

"I love you, too, sweetie," she yells back, turning to look at me one last time, her expression full of love, and I marvel how a single glance from my mother can feel like a shiny, protective shell all around me, as strong as the number 45 sunscreen I slather on my fair skin, the kind that won't let any of the bad stuff in.

ON SHAME

FATHER MARK ARRIVES AT OUR HOUSE FOR DINNER AND sits at the head of the table, opposite Father MacKinley. Sister June is here. The happy couple, Greenie and Luke, are here. Ash and Jada—who keep mouthing "Jamie Grant" every time I look at them—are here. Even Sister Mary Margaret from our parish has come—she told Mom she'd always wanted to meet the famous Catholic writer Father Mark Brendan, and my mother's attitude was the more the merrier. Mom has spent two entire days cooking and I feel guilty about not giving her more help, not offering suggestions of what to make, so guilty that I almost can't get anything down. This makes me feel even worse because she's already worried that I am not eating and here I am, doing it again. Pushing food around on my plate.

The only important person in my life absent tonight is Jamie. It's not that Mom didn't want him to come, but more that I knew his presence might make things awkward.

With Father Mark.

So I told Jamie it was a family-only dinner. In other words, I lied. I hate lying. But I'm getting good at it.

The discussion at the table is animated and everyone seems to be enjoying themselves. Everyone but me. I am uncomfortable. Unsettled. Unwilling to meet *his* eyes. I need to get away so I excuse myself and run upstairs to the bathroom.

I've had a glass of wine, something I never do, but my mother says it is a special occasion and so I drink it, but to tell the truth it makes me a bit dizzy. In the mirror I see a girl with tired eyes and no color in her cheeks and long straggly hair, and the internal voice that keeps talking to me lately wonders, *What's happening to you, Olivia?* and I do not have the answer so that's where the conversation ends.

When I step out of my bathroom I am not alone.

Father Mark stands in the entrance to my bedroom, his height reaching all the way to the top of the doorframe. His head bobs forward when he steps inside even though I have not invited him in and wasn't planning to. The first thought that pops into my head is that I am not allowed to have boys in my room, but this is inane and I'm upset it even crosses my mind in relation to Father Mark.

He is not a boy. He is a priest.

"Oh! Um, hi. *Hi.*" I tug at the hem of my sweater, not quite knowing how to handle his presence.

"Hello, Olivia," he says, as if we are just now seeing each other and haven't been seated together all evening. "I was looking for the bathroom."

"There's one down the hall to your left, just after the bookshelves." My tone is cheery, like a stewardess on an airplane giving directions. I wait, feeling awkward, wanting him to leave so I can get ahold of myself and rejoin the dinner party downstairs.

But Father Mark shows no sign of leaving.

My hands find my hair, twirling it around my fingers. I don't know what else to do or say. The distance I've been creating between us little by little over the past weeks has accumulated and grown into a wide gulf, a space that to me feels necessary. Essential. But awkward, too. This is extremely awkward because I can tell that it is a space he loathes. That makes him angry. He doesn't need to say a word.

I wish we could go back to the beginning and start over, do things differently.

"So this is where you sleep," Father Mark says, taking another step forward into this place that is mine, this place where I know he does not belong and where his eyes dart around, taking in my dresser, the rug, the windows, the closet, open, exposing my entire wardrobe. "And where you write," he adds, glancing at the coffee table in front of my couch, on top of which sits my laptop, closed, obvious, hidden yet in plain sight. He walks over to it, picks it up, moves to open it, which shocks me—as though he's grabbed my insides, squeezing them until I cannot breathe, and so I burst out, "Hey! Put that down! That's not yours!"

"Olivia." He sounds startled, disappointed, but he hangs on, his arms cradling my computer in front of him. "Friends don't keep secrets from each other."

"But my laptop, it's just not—"

He ignores my protest and flips it open, the light on the screen automatically coming to life.

"I said *NO!*" I shout, not quite understanding what has come over me—maybe the wine?—rushing over, yanking it away from him.

Father Mark is stunned, his face crushing with sadness, confusion, looking as if he's been punched.

So there we are, me hugging my laptop, safely closed, and Father Mark, looking at me, his eyes fixed on me, my body, his presence so strange, so dark against the vivid rose-colored backdrop of my room, a girl's room, a seventeen-year-old high school student's room, and my internal voice wanting to know, *What is he doing in here, Olivia?* and *Don't you see that something isn't right?*

"I'm sorry." Father Mark's voice fills with remorse. "I didn't mean to offend you. Really, I didn't."

My mouth opens but the words stay put. I turn my back to him, so he can no longer see my face.

"I didn't mean to intrude," he says.

"It's okay," I tell him, quiet, even though I don't know if this is true or if I'm just saying it to try to make the situation right. More questions scroll through my mind: *How did everything go from so wonderful and exciting to so awkward and uncomfortable?* and *What was the moment when it all changed?*

"Olivia." He hesitates, waits for me to encourage him, but I don't and he pushes on anyway. "I sense a change in you. Has something upset you? Did someone *do* something to you? Because if someone is bothering you—"

"No," I interrupt. "Everything is great."

"Good. That's good. A relief." He heaves a deep sigh and I can tell he means what he says and that everything is going to be okay—at least he thinks so—and we are going to go back downstairs and finish dinner and all will be fine.

Then Father Mark exclaims in a voice that is loud and angry, "Olivia!"

I turn toward him and see that he is standing near the couch and in his hands is a stack of letters that he's plucked from the top of the pile, my Father Mark pile, and all of them are still sealed and I feel a combination of embarrassment—that he's discovered how much I've saved; and shame—that he has evidence that I do not appreciate his attention, that I am ungrateful, that I don't bother to read what he gives to me anymore; and fear, too, about what happens now.

"You haven't opened any of these?" In his voice is a combination of astonishment, hurt, and fury.

All the possible excuses I might offer scroll through me like a tickertape—*Greenie's wedding, friendship crises, Mom has me managing stuff at the house while she helps Greenie with the planning*—anything that would diffuse this situation, anything other than Jamie, because mentioning him might make everything worse somehow, and so I pick the most innocuous one and start to explain in a voice that is unnaturally animated. "Well, it's complicated. See, Ash and Jada—" But I stop short when I hear the sound of all those letters falling to the floor in a soft *shhhhh* as they slide this way and that in their disarray and he turns around.

Father Mark stares at me, his face a blank. Unreadable.

"I'll see you back at the table." He walks past me toward the door in a few long, quick strides. I hear him leave, his footsteps, *thump thump, thump thump thump* down the stairs, and I recall that when he appeared in my room he was looking for the bathroom and he seems to have forgotten this. Laughter, loud, raucous peals of happy laughter erupt upon his arrival back in the dining room and I think he must have made a joke, delighting my family and guests as he always does, delighting everyone he meets. When he wants to at least.

After I breathe, in, out, for a good long while, my laptop still pressed against my chest, I put it back on the coffee table, doing my best to avoid looking at the Father-Mark-mess on the floor and make my way down to the dinner party where Father Mark immediately sends a warm smile in my direction and raises his glass and says something about me but I don't know what. I'm not listening. He acts as if nothing happened, nothing at all. I sit down, Father Mark to my right.

"Jack," Father Mark says, addressing Father MacKinley across the table. "Did you hear the news from St. Theresa's?"

"I did," Father MacKinley says, looking stricken. "It's so sad what has happened to our Church. Especially in Boston."

"I read about it in the bulletin this week," my mother says. "I think it's terrible."

"What is it?" Greenie sounds concerned.

"Another parish closing its doors." Mom shakes her head in sadness.

"Why?" I ask because I want to be involved in the conversation—I *need* to so no one thinks anything is wrong—and because I also genuinely want to know. It would be awful to lose our parish, Father MacKinley, and the community along with it, which for so long has been a family to my family.

"Why does any parish close its doors today?" Luke huffs, sarcastic. Angry. "These people and their accusations of abuse. They're so righteous. They think it's their duty to expose the Church's 'sins' by bleeding it dry with lawsuits and destroying the priesthood in the process."

The anger in the room, from Greenie and Luke especially, is palpable. A part of me understands why they feel such pain, they are so invested, so Catholic, but I am startled, too, by the conviction of their disbelief, their lack of sympathy for the victims in this equation. I am upset by it.

"I don't think anyone will see the collar the same way ever again," Father MacKinley says, resigned. "We live in a different era now. Priests aren't regarded as they used to be." The sadness in Father MacKinley's eyes—sadness mixed with kindness—seeing it makes me want to weep and I can't help but wonder, *How could anybody ever accuse someone like him?* because it is simply unimaginable. Impossible that he would do something so awful.

I look around and notice that everyone has stopped eating. Even Ash and Jada. Each of us look back and forth between Father MacKinley and Father Mark, like at a tennis match, watching the two priests in the two collars, conspicuous now at either end of the table.

Father Mark takes a sip of wine. "I've spoken to the Bishop about the situation."

"And?" Father MacKinley sounds hopeful.

"The Diocese of Boston keeps my royalties in a trust." Father Mark takes another sip, dabbing the side of his mouth with his napkin. "That's how Olivia's contest is funded." He pauses, smiling at me, and my stomach churns. "But I've asked that they open the account to parishes in danger of closing. After all, it's not as if I have any use for the money and it's a waste to the faithful just sitting there. St. Theresa's might be the first parish to benefit."

"Oh, Father! That is so generous." Mom beams.

"It's priests like you that will help our Church get back on its feet," Luke states with conviction.

"Mark, what a good thing you've done for that community. What a wonderful idea." Father MacKinley shakes his head, like he can't find the words to fully express his gratitude.

Greenie, on my left, leans forward, gazing at Father Mark like he's some kind of hero, and I notice that everyone else does the same—Luke, Mom, Father MacKinley, Sister Mary Margaret, Ash, and Jada. They are absorbed in his every word, drawn to him as if he is a magnet.

And I know what they feel. I've felt his pull, too. From the very first moment.

Only Sister June is unmoved. She looks at me now, looks at me hard, like she's trying to see something, find something in my eyes.

"It's really nothing," Father Mark says, deflecting the adoration flowing toward him, though I can tell he's enjoying it. "Let's turn toward happier subjects. I'm sorry I brought up something so dark at what's supposed to be a party for my protégé."

I force a laugh, feeling self-conscious when everyone turns to look at me when Father Mark calls me "his" as if I am a possession. *His* possession. Again I meet Sister June's eyes, her eyes searching mine, and a lightbulb switches to *on* and for a moment I am blinded by doubt and terror and the unfinished questions *could I, am I, is Father Mark, is he?* emerge from somewhere buried deep, but before they can become fully formed Jada steps in, taking Father Mark's comment as an invitation for funny Olivia anecdotes, and soon Ash joins her and the somber mood that has fallen across the dinner party lightens up again. Waves of relief wash over me, relief that Jada saves me from following those questions to their end, and the light that went on so bright, so quickly, switches back to *off* and those horrible suspicions that make me a terrible person for even thinking them, half-alive as they are, *were*, scurry back into their hiding place, and I wish for them to never come out again. *Never.*

ON IRREPARABLE HARM

THE NEXT EVENING FATHER MARK AND I SIT NEXT TO each other on chairs that are tightly packed into this intimate space where everyone listens with rapt attention to James McDaniel, the famous Irish writer, memoirist, who reads from his newest work of creative nonfiction.

I clap along with the rest of the audience in between one selection and the next.

The celebration is invitation only, which Father Mark kept reminding me in the car on our way here, but I don't realize how exclusive, how fancy it is until we arrive. I feel strange to be among the chosen, the writers, editors, publishers, and professors, the Boston intellectual elite, in this beautiful room with its glittering wall sconces, its shelves that reach the ceiling packed with the rarest of rare books, the Persian carpet soft, luxurious under our feet, and the air with its musty smell of greatness and history.

I don't belong here. I am out of place. Too young, too inexperienced. Too insignificant. I haven't earned the right to a spot in this room.

Father Mark's arms rest one on each thigh, parallel to his legs, his hands gripping his knees. McDaniel's voice, his words are released into the room one after the other like a strand of pearls, and Father Mark turns to look at me sitting in the antique wooden chair next to him, the chair with the curved armrests on which I refuse to rest even an elbow. I don't understand or listen to McDaniel and only my ears alert me that he is speaking because I am concentrating on the hem of my dress, how it doesn't quite cover my knees when I sit, and how the capped sleeves leave my arms almost bare. I should have dressed differently, more appropriately, worn a suit, a pantsuit, even though it is late June and hot and sticky and I don't even own a pantsuit but I should have bought one for tonight. Instead of professional and appropriate I feel yet again like a girl, a little girl at her first communion, a girl in a frilly party dress among the adults who know better, who are learned and wise, who must know something that I don't know because what I do know is that something isn't right, though I can't put my finger on it, can't quite articulate what *it* is.

What *is* it?

The other thing of which I am painfully, uncomfortably aware is that I am here by the grace of Father Mark D. Brendan, as his guest—this he does not let me or anyone else forget. Over and over, he says to everyone who stops to say hello to him, to congratulate him on this or that most recent award he's won, "This is Olivia Peters. She is here with me, as my guest." They smile, shake my hand, and then walk away. As if they *know*. As if they are uncomfortable with my presence, too. This lack of belonging, *my* lack of belonging, registers fully as McDaniel continues to read, each word adding another pearl onto the long, glamorous strand that I can not appreciate in this moment, though I wish, I *wish* I could.

Something is very wrong.

I look over at Father Mark, I study his face, his chin tilted slightly upward, his eyes, closed now, as if to better hear the words traveling toward us from the podium. On his lips, a smile. He seems enraptured. A chandelier hangs overhead and he is bathed in soft light, the top of his thick hair turned silver under a cascade of crystal.

His eyes pop open and in less than a blink he turns to me, catches me staring, watching. Instead of being flustered or even annoyed he is gleeful to see I have been taking him in, and his smile broadens until it is almost frightening.

I am frightened. Father Mark frightens me. This is what is wrong.

This.

In this moment—this very particular moment, with me reddening and him smiling—I see something a tad sinister in his eyes, calculating, measuring, *appraising* me like I am a bauble, a jewel with karats, clarity, cut, a *possession.* Something moves inside me, turns to ice, and a small, cold bead of warning lodges itself in the bottom curve of my heart and I think, *How have I not noticed this before?* and *Maybe I didn't allow myself to* and *Why did it take me so long to see?*

"What's the matter, Olivia?" he whispers, leaning close, so close I can feel his breath on my ear, reminding me of Jamie and his breath on my cheek and my neck, and I want to shove Father Mark away because he should not remind me of anything having to do with Jamie because Jamie he is not and I don't want memories of Jamie tainted with Father Mark. But his hand, Father Mark's hand, brushes across the back of my dress, and his hair presses slightly into mine.

I can feel it. All of it. It is all so clear.

And I freeze, determined not to move. It would be weird to shift away, like he was doing something other than simply asking whether I am okay. Then he would know I know something is wrong, if I move away. So I stay still, feel his warm breath, his body leaning toward mine, and I whisper, "Nothing, nothing at all, Father Mark," and he whispers, "Good," and sits back upright, closing his eyes again, enraptured again, by the reading.

Is it really the reading that has enraptured him? Taken him?

I sit there, next to Father Mark, wishing away this reading, this event that I was supposed to love, soak up, feel lucky to attend. I cannot lose myself in the words or the moment or Father Mark's presence, *because* of his presence. I want to bolt, run away, run as fast as I can as far as I can but I don't. Leaving would be strange, would call attention to that sharp-edged, frosty crystal that has taken up residence in my heart.

When McDaniel stops reading and the questions finally stop coming and everyone gets up and there is a reception, I stay because I've no other choice even though what I want is to go home. I think about calling a cab but decide it would be too conspicuous. I am afraid to call attention, to make everything worse than it already is, and Father Mark is my ride and I know, I know he will be upset and offended if I leave in a cab. So I smile and I mingle and I try to remember that these people are wonderful connections and Father Mark introduces me like I am some rising star and I know I should feel grateful, I should feel gratitude, I know I should, but for some reason this time, this awkward feeling and wishing I am elsewhere doesn't go away and what I do feel isn't anything resembling gratitude at all.

I plead with myself, *Olivia, you are wasting this opportunity and for what? Some indescribable feeling you get when Father Mark smiles? That is just plain stupid, Olivia.* I swallow this advice and try to pull myself together and nod thank you when I get congratulations and someone compliments me on my dress, the dress I wish I had not worn because it makes me stand out among everyone else in the room and the last thing I want is to be noticeable, and worse, noticeable in a girlish way, but there you have it.

Finally, after what seems like hours, it is over.

Time to go.

"Come on, Olivia," Father Mark says, turning to me, smiling again, a smile I don't want to read because I don't want to know what lurks behind it or how to understand its meaning. "Let's go to the car so I can get you home." He looks at his watch, pulling back his black shirtsleeve. "You have work to do, I'm sure."

"Yeah," I say, mustering a small laugh. "Of course," I say, forcing myself to sound enthusiastic even if my enthusiasm about my writing, about *him*, is not just faltering anymore but gone.

We get to his car, his modest car given him by the church, and he opens the passenger door for me.

"After you," he says, which immobilizes me for a second, because I don't like the sound of this or the order of things, and wish he would just get into his side of the car first and not let me in like it's some, like it's a . . . I don't know. I just don't like this.

In the car, on the ride home, I am silent.

Father Mark, though, he talks. He talks about the classical

music that plays on the CD, with its beautiful, haunting cello and violin, telling me how he thought I would like it, that he chose it especially for me, that he knew I'd be in the car and he wanted me to listen to it, that when he listens to this piece in particular he thinks of me.

As the strings sing their melancholy notes I want to disappear, to become invisible. I want to press Eject, take the CD and break it in two. Instead, I count the blocks and shut out his voice, his comments, his romantic classical music that makes him think of me. Three . . . two . . . one more block and we are idling in front of my house.

"Thank you," I say, without looking at him, avoiding his gaze, opening the door to let myself out, to welcome the warm, humid air that already sticks to the right side of my body, my foot on the sidewalk, telling myself, cheering myself, that I am almost home. "I'll see you in class."

His hand grabs my left arm, holding me, stopping me from leaving.

I stop, pause, wait. *Maybe he'll just let go.* But he doesn't. His grip burns.

"Olivia! Look at me." A demand, not a request.

One foot on the sidewalk, one foot still inside the car, I give up and turn to him.

In his hand is an envelope, a manila envelope. He takes a deep breath. "What I have for you is something very dear to me. A story. A special one. My newest. Still unpublished. In fact, I've just written it, very quickly, over the last few weeks. No one else has seen it—"

"I hope your editor loves it," I interrupt, trying to stop him from continuing.

He is undaunted.

"—and I wish you to read it. I want to discuss it soon. I *need* you to read this—"

Needs me to?

"—it is very important to me, that you do this. Do you understand?"

I say nothing.

"Olivia!" *Oh-liv-ee-aah!*

I do nothing.

But his hands, rough, violent, they push, shove, force the envelope at me. It sits there for a second, against my body, threatening to slide to the ground before I grasp it and turn away.

"Olivia," he says again because he won't stop saying my name. Refuses to. "Promise me you'll read it."

I nod yes.

"Promise me out loud," he commands.

But I don't. Won't.

"I'll see you in class," I say, and get out of the car, feeling suffocated, dying to get into the house and out of his view and to stop, by all means, stop any contact, praying with every fiber of my being that he'll forget about me, drop this charade, and *just let me go*.

I do not want any more of it. Of this. Of *him*.

This I know. I know this now. I am certain.

I refuse to look back, to wave at him from the front door, though I hear the sound of his car idling, waiting, watching for me to disappear inside.

The house is dark when I enter. I flip on light after light after light, wanting to be surrounded by light, feeling frightened, scared of the dark, of the darkness everywhere, seeping into me, so I leave a trail of light after me as I make my way through the house.

When I reach my bedroom I toss the envelope onto the pile with the rest of it, the small mountain between my couch and the sill, still messy and untouched after Father Mark's tantrum at dinner. I put on my pajamas, get into bed and burrow under the covers because I want to be buried, protected, hidden. I try to will myself to sleep but tugging at the corner of my consciousness is the story, his story, sitting so close that I cannot forget that it is there. A part of me wants to know what's inside, to get it over with, to read it because I have a sense . . . I think it might . . . but then the biggest parts of me say, *Olivia, don't go there, just don't.* So maybe in the end I'll get out of reading it like I get out of everything else recently, because he'll start to get the picture like anyone else would, with him so desperate to be in touch and me avoiding, resisting, running away, because I will not stop avoiding. I will not. And eventually he will understand and stop and there will be no confrontation, no need for one, and then everything will be okay again because how could he not get the picture with all the signals I'm sending? How could he not? He will, in time he will eventually. My mother is always saying that *patience is a virtue* and I determine that I can ride this out, that I can be patient and virtuous, and so in the end no harm will have to come to anyone. *Patience, Olivia, patience,* I repeat over and over until sleep finally claims me.

✤ I I I ✤

I do so much want to love her as we began,
spiritually—I do believe such spiritual love is not
only possible but does exist between us, deeply,
purely, strongly, and the rest can be controlled.
Yet she is right to be scared. We can simply
wreck each other.

—THOMAS MERTON

ON PRESSURE

JUNE TURNS INTO JULY AND I THROW MYSELF INTO EV-
erything that comes my way—everything that has nothing to
do with Father Mark. Addressing Greenie's invitations, planning
her shower, spending time with Ash and Jada, and Jamie, I see
more and more and more of Jamie. Jamie who makes me forget.
I want as much Jamie as possible. I wish for a brain that thinks
only Jamie-thoughts because Jamie is the one person who can pull
me out of the darkness that has settled over me, into me, through-
out every part of me because of *him*. I am a heavy, dark cloud
creeping across the sidewalks and parks of Boston, always bring-
ing with me doom and gloom and destroying everyone's mood
around me, about to rain and ruin everything and everyone nearby.

And now, now, *now* I wish with all my heart that I had never
won this stupid freaking writing contest which is what got me
into this mess with Father Mark who is probably going to call
any minute because he calls just about *every* minute if he's not
e-mailing or texting every other minute or racing after me when
class is over to discuss his stupid story only to find out that

I, the ungrateful Olivia Peters, have still so far only read the title.

This Gorgeous Game. By Mark D. Brendan.

I can't bring myself to go any further.

I attend class to keep up appearances and because, well, Jamie is there and we go together and because if I stop going people will wonder *why* and *what happened* and say things like *That's not like you, Olivia, to skip class* and *Olivia, you used to be so excited about it* and then I will have to come up with something to say. More and more and more reasons *why* and *why not* and for now going seems the path of least resistance, to just get in, get out, get home, and quick—at least until I find a better solution or it all stops and the situation resolves itself.

I want this situation to resolve itself.

As it is, Jamie knows something is up. That something is going on. That something is wrong. He's started to make leading remarks like *Wow, Father Mark calls you a lot, doesn't he?* and *Father Mark is always leaving you things* and *You realize that Father Mark treats you different than everyone else, right?* and all of these oblique observations require me to make even more excuses, to become a full-time Father Mark Excuse Machine because it's only a matter of time before Father Mark gets the picture and stops, before it all stops and goes away, and if I can just keep this up a little longer then everything will be okay.

I have to believe this.

The other option is unthinkable. It requires that I . . . that I . . . and I can't. I just can't.

Please, God. Please fix this for me.

On yet another class day when the clock says three p.m. I drag myself from my room and out of the house, all the while debating whether or not to skip, to give myself a reprieve, engage in this internal tug of war—*To go or not to go? To go or not to go?*—always, eventually, landing on *go* because if I go I will see Jamie and I will avoid raised eyebrows from other parties. But most of all I won't set *him* off because God only knows how badly I want to avoid doing that, giving Father Mark cause to come after me in some other new and creative way, and at least, at least if he sees me in class it seems to satisfy him somehow, pacify him, keep him from using that imagination for other purposes.

It's amazing, the things he thinks of doing. Trying.

But today, today for some reason I remember that I can see Jamie after class or tomorrow, since by now Jamie always wants to see me as much as I want to see him, and I've only gone as far as the sidewalk in front of my house, my feet like lead, before I flip open my cell—three more missed calls to add to the four from earlier. I find Jamie's number and hit Send.

I decide to give myself a pass.

"Olivia." Jamie picks up right away.

"Hi, Jamie," I say, and scrape my foot back and forth along the cement. I can't help but smile when I hear Jamie's voice and the gloom lifts a little.

"What's up? Are you on your way?"

"I was calling about class. I'm not going."

"Oh."

There is disappointment in that "Oh." And a silence that follows.

"Are you sick?"

"No. I just have a lot of stuff to do. For Greenie. For Greenie's wedding." I hate lying to Jamie.

"Olivia."

"Jamie." I mimic his serious tone, trying to lighten things up.

"Is there something you aren't telling me?"

Here we go again.

"What do you mean?" I play dumb, stabbing at the sidewalk with the toe of my shoe.

"I'm not sure. I know it hasn't been that long since we've been seeing each other but I feel like we've gotten really close. But then I sense you are holding something back. Something important." He sighs. "I want you to be able to tell me anything, Olivia. Absolutely anything."

No you don't, I think. *Not this, you don't.*

"I trust you," I say, and lean against a car parked along the street. The metal burns hot through my T-shirt even though the sun is hidden behind some clouds.

"Olivia."

"I do," I say, and wait another long moment. "So I'll see you tomorrow at three?"

I hear him breathing, in, out, hesitation, then resignation. "Fine. All right. Let's meet at our spot," he says, which makes my heart beat quicker. Jamie and I have "a spot" like other couples have "a song" and it's the bench in the Public Garden. We go there almost every day now, ever since that first night of class. "I'll be around later tonight online if you want to chat," he adds.

"Good to know."

"Well. Maybe talk to you later then," he says, and I hear the phone click on the other end.

I look up at the darkening sky and see that it's probably about to storm like it does sometimes on summer afternoons, the thunder and lightning and rain rolling in and out over the course of an hour. The phone vibrates and I pick up without thinking. "What, you miss me already?"

"Olivia," scolds a familiar voice, and not the one I was expecting to hear. "I've been trying to reach you for days."

I slide down the side of the car until I'm sitting on the sidewalk.

"Olivia? Are you there?"

"Hi, Father Mark. Sorry. I, um, I thought you were someone else."

"Olivia, what is going on with you?" He is urgent. Desperate.
How is it that I've made him so desperate? Why?

"Nothing. Everything is fine. I'm fine."

"Then you should call me back. I've left so many messages."

"My voice mail isn't working," I lie. "And my cell is acting up."

"You should get it fixed."

"Yeah."

"I've left messages with your mother, too."

"She must have forgotten to tell me."

"That doesn't sound like her."

Just because you've met my mother a few times doesn't mean you know her, I want to say. "Well. We've been busy. Family stuff."

Silence on the other end. Then, "I'm glad I caught you."

I wait for him to continue. I already know what comes next.

"Have you read it yet?" *The* story. *His* story. He is irritated and hopeful at once.

"No," I tell him for the millionth time, wanting to scream, wondering why and how our every interaction went from being about *my* story to talking about *his* freaking story, and when I can't even bring myself to get beyond page one. So I go into excuse mode. "It's just, I've got so much going on . . . a lot of . . . stuff . . . at home . . . with my sister's wedding. I'm sorry," I say, but the only thing I am really sorry about is picking up my cell without looking at the caller ID.

"Olivia." His voice is cold. "This is unacceptable behavior," he says, sounding like a father. "It's almost unforgivable."

Almost? Please. Don't forgive me and let's part ways.

He waits for me to say something. Rain begins to fall. Fat, heavy drops.

"Olivia?"

"I'm here." Big splotches of water polka dot the sidewalk, the front walk. Me. Plop. Splash.

"We need to talk in person. Wait for me after class tonight," he orders.

"Sure. I will." I lie.

"I want you to promise me, Olivia, that you'll wait."

"I promise." My voice is a whisper. I have to push the words out of my mouth.

"It's not nice to break promises, Olivia."

"I know." Tears well and mix with the rain rolling down my cheeks. Off the tip of my nose. Warm drops of water mat my hair and pool in the fold of my T-shirt near my stomach.

"Good. I'm glad we understand each other." He sounds excited. Relieved. "Now, the next thing—"

"Oh look, there's the T train coming. Gotta go. See you later," I interrupt and shut the phone. Click.

I tilt my head forward, between my knees. My hair falls in a wet curtain around me. The only thing that gets me up off the ground and running into the house is the knowledge that if I shut myself in my bedroom right away, then when Mom emerges from her study she might not notice that I am there, skipping class. At least not for a while. I shut the front door behind me, catching a quick glance of myself in the long mirror on the foyer wall, thinking *pathetic* when I see the girl reflected back, the Olivia I've become. I am soaked through and water drips from my hair, my face, my clothes and onto the floor. But then a surge of relief runs through me about not having to see Father Mark tonight and a burst of energy gets me bounding up the stairs into my room and onto my couch, tucked into the comfort of a warm blanket that I wrap around myself, all the way up to my eyes.

My consolation is short-lived, however, because as soon as I peer out, letting the soft shield fall to my chin, I see the manuscript on the coffee table. I can't bring myself to lift my arms to turn it over. To touch it.

This Gorgeous Game. By Mark D. Brendan.

I look away. Burrow deeper under the afghan again.

I try to forget the now and the how I got here and the moment it all started and how I walked right off a ledge I didn't even realize was there and before I knew it, before I was even the tiniest bit aware I was falling, falling fast, and now there is nothing I can do. Nothing I can do but fall and wait, fall and await the impact. When is the impact coming? I wonder. Or is this it? Is it slow and painful and never-ending?

I glance at the pile of letters and other memorabilia between the couch and the windowsill, the Father Mark loot I was once so proud to have acquired. One last ray of sun falls across it as the afternoon fades to night, as if God wants to remind me it is all there, the spoils of my naïveté, my stupidity, my trusting nature.

Sometimes I hate God. I just do.

ON A KISS

THE NEXT DAY IS THE HOTTEST ON RECORD. THE THER-mometer rises past 100 degrees and keeps on going. The light-ning storms that rumbled through Boston during the night made everything wet. Heavy. Steam rises from puddles scattered along the pavement. Droplets of water hang in the air and I swim, not walk, through it. A thick haze blankets everything, muting the sun's light.

I glance around Arlington Avenue, uneasy, wishing it was al-ready time to meet Jamie. Maybe it's just the heat. People mill about the park, tourist families making the requisite visit to the Public Garden to see the ducks and the swans. My cell says two o'clock. Mom wouldn't let me leave the house without it, said she's tired of not being able to reach me and she's tired of hav-ing to force me to eat, too, tired of my excuses—that my stomach hurts, that my phone isn't working right. She found my cell on the top shelf of the kitchen cabinet last night, long after I'd gone to bed, long after we fought about why I was home and not in class, and why, if I wasn't feeling well, I was refusing all the help and comfort she had to offer—tea, soup, toast, talk.

"Why in the world would you put your phone there, Olivia?" she wanted to know this morning when I came downstairs, still in my pajamas, but I just shrugged and took it from her. "What's gotten into you, Olivia?" she asked but I didn't have a good answer so I didn't say anything.

At the gates to the park, I debate what to do since Jamie won't be here for another hour. A bead of sweat drips down my back and I tug my shirt away from my body.

My mouth is dry—is it nerves? The walk here? The heat?

I need a drink, something icy to enjoy while I wait for Jamie. Even though on principle I am against Starbucks, they are on practically every corner so I head for the nearest one.

Cold air rushes to greet me when I open the door and for a brief moment I decide I love Starbucks because the frigid air is such a relief from this heat. It's packed, people everywhere reading the paper, hanging out with friends, chatting, pairs of moms drinking their coffees with strollers squeezed between tables. Half the customers are typing away at laptops, and I wonder, *Do I even want this anymore? To be a writer? To sit with my laptop like some novelist?* I push these thoughts away and head up the line to place my order.

After paying for an iced latte I stand by the counter, watching the man at the espresso machine whip up what seems like ten drinks at once. Customers wipe sweat from their brows, pulling at their shirts. That's why they keep it so cold in here, I think, so people can tolerate steaming coffee on even the hottest summer days.

Tap, tap goes my foot, impatient. I pace in the small space where you wait, grab a few napkins, a stirrer, decide I'm not ready to go back out into the heat yet, look around for a vacant table. I see a woman with a baby starting to get up, packing her things, the very same moment the world starts spinning. A tornado in my head.

The espresso man calls out my drink and I force myself to walk up to the counter. Nausea ricochets off the walls of my stomach like it wants to punch holes. I try to focus. Grab the coffee and run. Run fast.

Run, Olivia, run.

My body ignores these commands.

"Olivia!" The surprise is fake. So obviously fake. "How ser-endipitous to run into you here, especially after not seeing you yesterday. I am very, *very* upset about this business of you skipping class." He lets this last bit cross me like a threatening shadow.

Father Mark.

Come on, Olivia. Act normal. This is not a big deal. Don't make this more painful than it needs to be. He's just a person. Just a professor. Just a priest. Person, professor, priest. Person, professor, priest. I am locked in the center of a Father Mark triangle, walls all around me, and him everywhere I turn. There is no way out.

I focus on the soothing cold of the drink in my hand, force a smile onto my face.

"Hi, Father," I say, and can't help but notice how good I've become at forcing enthusiasm. So skilled at this game of pretend, of cat and mouse. "Getting a drink on your way to HMU?" In my voice is hope, hope that this will be over quick.

"Oh look, there's a table opening up over there. Why don't you grab it while I order my coffee. Then I'll join you and we can finally have a conversation." He sounds exasperated. "We need to talk, Olivia," he says.

My feet obey and carry my body along to the table, but everything else is numb. Slow. Surreal. How did my Jamie anticipation hour turn into coffee with Father Mark? Did he know I was going to be here? How would he?

Unless . . . unless . . .

No. No, no, no, no.

This is not happening. Not to me. *Not to me.* The suspicions, those unfinished questions that keep threatening to emerge from where I keep pushing them, to deeper and darker places each time, the—*could I, am I, is Father Mark, is he?*—one of them sneaks out from hiding and completes itself before I can stop it, and then the others, they snowball.

Is Father Mark, is he one of those *priests? Am I a . . . a . . . ?*

But then, as if shoving something down into the garbage with all my might, I trash these thoughts by focusing on the following, glaring, obvious fact: Father Mark has done nothing . . . nothing other than . . . I stop. Complete the sentence. *Father Mark has never laid a finger on me. At least not like that.*

Conclusion: *I am making something out of nothing. Literally.*

Just breathe, Olivia. Everything is totally fine. Sit, Olivia. Sit down. You'll feel better. Stop making things melodramatic. It's just coffee. *Coffee.* He's just an awkward man, a man who has a difficult time getting the picture, a man who probably doesn't hear *no* very often and so he is not used to it and so it takes him longer to understand because after all, he is Father Mark D. Brendan and people treat him more like he's a celebrity than a Catholic priest.

Soon Father Mark pulls out the other chair to sit and places his coffee on the table. A cappuccino, whole milk, no sugar. I know this because before this game of avoidance started we had many coffees together. Too many to count. *Remember, Olivia,* I tell myself, *coffee is harmless.* This is all harmless.

Father Mark talks and I have no idea what he is saying.

All of a sudden there is a lull in the conversation. I snap out of my daze and nod my head to indicate I am listening even though I am not listening.

"Olivia," He says, and looks at me, those big eyes intense, and I see anger in them, just a flash, but it's there. What have I done now? All the energy leaves my body. I am deflated. I want to put my head down on the table to rest, close my eyes, but I can't. Won't. Don't want to be that close. He's waiting, waiting, but for what? What is he waiting for me to say? Do? "Olivia." Again he says my name. Expectant. Expecting what, I don't know.

"Sorry, what? I must've zoned out for a second. Having trouble sleeping lately," I explain, hoping it's enough. Hoping he'll accept my excuse.

"My story, Olivia." *Oh-liv-ee-aah* goes my name from his mouth yet again, like chalk screeching against a blackboard, and I can't believe there was a time when it sounded like music to my ears, the way he says my name. "We need to talk about it, Olivia. I don't understand why you keep avoiding this conversation!" His voice gets louder, his tone borders on hysterical.

What can I do to calm him down?

Please, God, make him calm down!

My eyes dart left, right, down at the tall plastic cup in front of me, empty except for ice. I sucked it dry without noticing. Needles prickle my skin, a wave up my arms and down my back. Say something. Tell him you don't want to read the damn freaking story. You won't. You can't. You *refuse*. That you want *nothing, nothing, nothing* more from him, no more of him, nothing ever again, that this is over, over. *Over.* This game is over.

End. Of. Discussion.

But I don't say any of this. Instead I ask, "Why do you need me to read it so badly? Why is this so important to you?"

Tell me why! Give me something to go on! Say something real! Say it out loud!

Father Mark says nothing. There is a long silence. Then a statement. "You haven't read it yet."

I shake my head no.

"Good to know where your priorities are, Olivia," Father Mark says in not at all a nice way, knuckles rapping the table. "Between this and missing class, I don't know what to make of this anymore. Maybe I made a mistake with you. Maybe I was wrong about you, about what you could handle. What you were ready for. There were so many others I could have chosen . . ." His voice trails off and I cannot tell who these "others" are, the ones that are the object of his statement—other people who entered the contest, or just . . . *others* . . . and chosen for what exactly? What did he really choose me for? "Think about what you are doing. What you are throwing away."

"But I just—"

"Olivia." *Oh-liv-ee-aah.*

My eyes bore into my lap, the bottom of the cup cold on my thighs.

"If there is only one thing that you do for me, Olivia . . ." He pauses, wanting me to feel the weight of his words, of the way he has handed me the world, *his* world on a platter, and I offer him nothing in return, lately, aside from playing hard to get. "You *must* read this story. *Please.*"

I look up. Blank stare. Panic.

It is just a story, Olivia. What is your problem?

"Olivia." *Oh-liv-ee-aah.*

"Um, I'm sorry. I'm really sorry . . . I . . . I . . . but I need to go." I get up, knocking the cup to the ground. The top pops off and ice spills onto the carpet. Father Mark bends down to pick it up and I jump back, out of his way.

Father Mark straightens, cup in hand, eyes wide, and sighs. Big blinking eyes. Big imposing man. Person. Professor. Priest. "I will try to be patient, Olivia. Besides, I have a responsibility to you, don't I? But in winning this contest *you* accepted a responsibility, too. To me, to the other contestants, to the future winners. You are a rare talent and here I am, watching you let yourself down. I don't understand why, but I feel obliged to stick with you, to push you when you need to be pushed. You know I am only trying to help, don't you? There are so many things I can do for you, for your future. I can *give* you a future, a future you said you wanted. Your dream, remember? Here I am handing it to you. Don't you want it? Don't you?"

"No . . . yes . . . I mean . . . I do. I do." I stutter, my voice so small, no louder than a pin dropping. "I appreciate everything you've done. I do."

I walk toward the exit. I want to run but force myself to walk. The minutes inch toward three o'clock. He trails after me. Follows me out the door. Walks beside me on the street in silence. We near the park where I am supposed to meet Jamie and I veer right instead, toward Sacred Heart.

"Olivia." *Oh-liv-ee-aah.*

"I will. I'll do it. Tonight. I'll read it. Okay? I promise."

Soon I am standing at the bottom of the steps of my high school chapel, as if I needed Father Mark to remember who I am, who he is talking to.

A high school girl. A seventeen-year-old girl.

"I've got to go," I tell him.

"You promise."

"Yee-esss." It comes out in two syllables.

"I'm going to call you later tonight and you *will* pick up the phone."

"Yes."

"Good. Wonderful!" He sounds so satisfied. "I look forward to it."

I stand there, staring ahead. He stands at my side, facing me, close. Too close. I don't look at him. I can't make myself.

"I've got to go," I say again, thinking about Jamie, how Jamie is waiting for me somewhere else, how he's going to think I stood him up, but I can't worry about that right now. I need to sit and think. Alone. People stream by us on the sidewalk, some happy, some complaining about the heat. "Bye," I say, turning away.

"Olivia . . ." he says one last time. I stop. Waiting. A few more stragglers pass. Moments elapse. Forever we stand there, unmoving. The street empties. Then the unthinkable.

Father Mark moves toward me. Next to me. Close. He leans forward and kisses me on the cheek. A kiss. A peck. A wet smack like some middle school boy, but the thing is Father Mark is not a seventh-grade boy. Not even close.

Oh. My. God.

In a flash he is gone, down the block, almost in a run, his long, confident strides carrying him quick, around the corner and out of sight.

I stand there, sick, unable to move. My cheek wet. Feeling disgust. Repulsion. A churning stomach.

Calm down, Olivia. It was just a peck. On the cheek. No big deal.

But I replay it over and over. My legs give way and I clutch the banister, a cold, metal life preserver on the stairway to a house of God. God help me. God keep me from drifting into oblivion. God please. God, please stop this, whatever *this* is. He's *yours* after all. He's your responsibility so fix this. Fix it!

Minutes pass. By now Jamie is sitting on the bench at our spot alone, waiting for me, and I am not going to show. I pull myself up the steps. Breathe. Deep breaths. One foot in front of the other, I head into the chapel. A Catholic chapel. A Catholic church. *How ironic to seek solace here,* I think, as the heavy door shuts with a loud thud behind me.

ON PRAYER

WHY, GOD? WHY ME?

The old wood of the pew creaks under my weight. Everything slows. My brain. My heart. I set the kneeler down gently, so it doesn't make a sound. My forehead rests on the rail of the bench in front of me. I wish everything would stop. Even for a few moments. Turning my head to the side I stare up at the tall window nearby. Yellow, red, and orange slivers of glass surround Mary and bathe her in light. The royal blue of her robe sparkles. Her arms reach out and up, and for a moment I believe she could take this heavy feeling from me, take it and give it to God. Save me from carrying it any longer.

The chapel is empty and dark, save for the filtered rays of sun that leave a colorful glow along the ends of the pews, and the occasional station of lit candles, flames flickering.

My knees begin to ache and I sit back onto the bench, staring at the altar. I try to imagine what I've been told all my life is real, that God loved us enough to become human, to be closer to us, to walk among us. That a Catholic priest stands in for this

God-become-human among the faithful and is treated like God come down from heaven by them, too. By us. By me. Ever since I was a little girl.

Though I don't know that I can count myself among them anymore. The thought of losing this faith, my place in this church that has been with me and everyone I love all my life, feels like facing an earthquake, one that might swallow me into the ground and take me away from Greenie and Luke, my mom. Maybe even Jamie. I don't want to lose them. I don't want to betray all of these people. Father MacKinley. It doesn't seem fair.

I can't. It's unimaginable.

"I'm surprised to see you here, Olivia."

I spin around. Sister June is standing in the aisle, watching me.

"I didn't mean to scare you." Her voice is soft. "Can I sit with you awhile?"

"Okay," I say.

Sister June slides into the pew, a rustle of fabric against wood. She doesn't speak. Just sits near enough that I am aware of her presence. Minutes tick by. I feel the need to explain why I am here. "I needed to think," I say without turning my head.

"Is everything okay?" The sound of her voice is quiet amid the vaulted ceilings, the wooden buttresses above.

"Sure. I think so. Am I not supposed to be here? I know school is technically closed. But I wanted to come to a place where I felt comfortable. Safe. And I ended up here. Are you going to—"

"I came here to pray. So no." She turns to me. "I'm not going to tell you to leave."

"Am I in trouble?"

"Are you?" Her eyes fill with concern. "What are you not telling me, Olivia?"

"Nothing. Nothing at all. Everything is fine," I lie. I lie because I just . . . I have to.

Sister June's face fills with skepticism. She puts one sensible, thick rubber-soled shoe onto the kneeler—I always get yelled at for doing that—and crosses her legs, her tan skirt just long enough to cover her calves.

"Can you hear confessions?" I hear myself asking.

"It depends how you mean, Olivia," she says, hands clasped in her lap, eyes turning from me to gaze up at the altar. "You've been at Sacred Heart long enough—since when, kindergarten?—to know that only priests can perform the sacraments."

"I know, but I thought maybe—"

"There are no exceptions. We are Catholic, dear." She chuckles.

"What if there is something I don't feel comfortable telling a man? I mean, it doesn't seem fair that we can only go to priests. There are certain things that I don't think men can really understand, or be unbiased about." I stop, before revealing anything more.

"Technically you are confessing your sins to God when you confess to a priest. But believe me, I know it doesn't always seem that way. Or *ever* seem that way." Sister June sighs. "I try to keep this in mind, though, every time I go to confession—that ultimately whatever I say is between me and God."

"I don't think that will work right now," I say, and wonder whether Father Mark goes to confession, if he has told anyone what he does, if he goes daily, confessing then getting absolved, confession then absolution, over and over and over and *over and over and over* so he can do it again, free of guilt. God's forgiveness at my expense. Wouldn't his confessor think something is wrong? Do something to stop him from continuing? Or is it that nothing is wrong at all? That it's only in my head? Maybe Father Mark doesn't even think about it. Maybe it never occurs to him that he has anything to confess. Maybe I am being melodramatic.

"Olivia, if there is anything you want to tell me, you can tell me in confidence. I cannot absolve you of whatever it is you want to be free from—I do not have that formal capacity. But I can listen. I am here. I'm not just a teacher or your principal. I minister to anyone in need. I've known you since you were small and if anything was wrong, *is* wrong, I would want you to tell me. I wouldn't want you to go through anything alone," she says, turning to face me, the creaking wood loud in the quiet sanctuary. She lays a hand on my shoulder. "No one should ever feel alone in their pain and worry and you are no exception. You are *never* alone."

Tears spring to my eyes and I wipe them away. They leave a wet trail across my cheek.

"You can always tell God, Olivia. You can pray to God. God is always there for us. I believe that."

"What if I don't want God to know, either? What if I don't want anyone to know?" My voice is barely audible. A knot expands in my throat.

"You never have to keep anything from God. I promise. God will love you no matter what. God can help." A sob.

"What if God's the problem? What if it's God's fault?"

"Oh, Olivia. Can't you tell me what's wrong? I'm so worried."

"I can't," I whisper. "It's probably nothing."

With gentle hands Sister June takes both of my shoulders, shifting so she can look straight into my eyes. More tears, big tears, pour down my face and I realize this is the first time I've let myself cry over this in front of someone else. "Olivia, I promise you, I promise that I will hear whatever you have to say. No one should bear the burden of our humanity alone. When you are ready to let me share that burden I will help you carry it. Do you understand me?"

"Yes." I want to believe her but also want to believe that I will never need what she offers.

"Can I pray for you now? Do you mind if I ask that God grant you help? I know that your faith is wavering but mine is not. I'd like to talk to God for you, okay?"

I manage a nod. Another sob convulses through my body. Sister June shifts onto the kneeler. I sit, unable to move. She leans into me as her body bends in prayer.

"God, please grant Olivia the grace she needs to walk through this difficult moment on her journey in this life. Please love Olivia with all the love that You are . . ." Sister June continues and I listen to her words, try to join her in asking God to intercede on my behalf. As much as Sister June's faith makes an impression, seeing this woman feel so powerful on behalf of such strong belief, I find I cannot pray with her. I cannot talk to God right now. I cannot utter one word or ask one thing on my behalf.

But Sister June can. Will. *Does.*

I can't help thinking that it's God's fault, it is God who did this, who brought this trouble into my life, this insurmountable problem that won't go away no matter how hard I try, no matter what I do or don't do. So instead, I begin to pray, silently, to Sister June, that her words are true. That if I ever decide I want to talk she will be there. That she will not judge me for what I say. Not like God might.

Not like *Him*.

Sister June and I sit there a long time, how long I have no idea. When I get up to leave she grabs my hand, squeezing it, as if she isn't ready for me to leave. As if she's waiting for something, waiting for me to say something. Eventually, after a while, she lets go, she lets me go and I walk up the aisle and through the doors and back out into the blistering July day.

ON GIVING IN

"OLIVIA . . . OLIVIA . . . *OLIVIA!*"

I am deaf. The voice falls on deaf ears. I make myself deaf to his voice. I can't believe this. This is not happening.

"Olivia!" *Oh-liv-ee-aah!*

He must have waited for me outside the chapel.

And now he is following me home.

He won't give up.

As if the kiss wasn't bad enough.

I refuse to turn around. I keep walking because I will not stop. Please. Don't. Make. Me. The sun's heat pulses in the hazy sky.

Footsteps thump behind me. Thump quickly. *Thump, thump, thump.*

"Olivia!" He is screaming. My name from his lips appears in the air, hangs there, big, loud, suspended for a moment, then disappears. Again and again, my name.

And this time, this time, I begin to run.

I run away from the writer I once idolized, as if he is no one special. I conjure the walls between us layered with vows, authority, professional obligations between professor and student, priest and girl. So many barriers. Sacred barriers, barriers not meant to be crossed, real and powerful. When I glance backward, see that he is still behind me, I pick up my pace, run so fast that my lungs scream in protest but I do not slow until I am all the way home, and the sight of our town house has never seemed so welcoming as it does now, and I am almost there. One foot in front of the other. I turn inside the gate, taking the front steps two at a time, and soon I am inside. Shut the door behind me and lean against it. *Click* goes the lock. Home safe.

"Olivia, is that you?" Mom calls out from the kitchen.

I go upstairs and into my room without answering her. I close the curtains, one by one, and my room blooms giant, exuberant red and pink peonies, the sun a soft rosy glow through the fabric. I lie down on the thick, grass-colored rug. Close my eyes. Catch my breath. Bathe myself in the light encircling me like a womb.

The door swings open and Mom's face peeks inside. "Are you sick again?" She sounds worried. "Sweetie, what has gotten into you?"

"Yes. I'm sick. I think I'm sick."

"Greenie is coming over tonight," Mom says as if this might help. "I hope you aren't getting the flu." She walks over and bends down to put her hand across my forehead to see if I am feverish. "You're flushed."

"I'm going to rest, okay? Maybe take a nap. I just need to be alone for a while."

"Okay." She is hesitant, worried. "If you need anything at all, just give a yell downstairs." She stands to leave, then stops. "Before I forget, this was left for you on the steps." She releases a small, square envelope from her hand, letting it fall on the floor next to me, and disappears before she can see me shrink away. Another letter. Something else from *him*. It barely whispers as it lands, sliding ever so slightly along the surface like a feather, so light, so unlike what I expect of something that feels like such a burden.

I don't touch it.

Instead I sit up and reach for my laptop under the couch, positioning it carefully across my legs. When my e-mail account comes up I write Jamie a quick message.

> Jamie, I'm sorry about today. Something came up and
> I couldn't make it. I'm not feeling well. Please know it
> has nothing to do with you. I'll explain

I stop typing. Will I explain? Will I really? I backspace, erasing this.

> I need some time to think.

I don't know how to sign it. *Best, Olivia? Love, Olivia?* Either option seems wrong, on the one hand too formal and on the other too much. I settle on something in between.

> xo, Olivia

I'm about to log off when an instant message pops up. I quickly shut down the computer. My cell phone comes to life. I'm careful not to touch it. When the ringing stops I grab it, shut it down, and push both my laptop and cell into the darkness underneath my couch.

What dominates my attention, my awareness, despite all ef-forts to ignore it, is the manuscript, Father Mark's story, sitting on my coffee table. Facedown. Tucked safely away in its manila envelope. I still haven't been able to bring myself to read beyond the title. To so much as touch it. But I promised. And it is just a pile of papers. A pile of papers with words on them. Words are just words. There is nothing to be afraid of, Olivia. Get it over with.

I reach for it, despite my repulsion. Fear. Anxiety.

I bend the metal hinge, open the flap, and let the thin manu-script slide into my hands.

And finally, after all this time, I begin to read.

·

ON REGRET

OH GOD. MY STOMACH CONTRACTS. PLEASE NO.

No, no, no.

I am imagining things. I have to be. I want to be.

His story is splayed across the floor of my room like a stain.

His confession.

I shouldn't have read it. I should've listened to my gut and my gut said *don't do it.* I want to take it back, I want to pull all of the words out of my head, but I can't.

What's done is done.

Oh God what have I done?

My gut tells me to run into the bathroom and this time I listen. I get down on my knees and lean my head over the toilet and begin to heave.

ON DARK NIGHTS
OF THE SOUL

I SLEEP RIGHT THROUGH DINNER AND GREENIE'S VISIT—
only vaguely aware when Mom comes in to check on me, to
ask if I want anything, to tell me that Father Mark is downstairs, but she'll tell him I'm sick, that I'm resting. He's staying
to eat with them, she explains, just in case I find the energy to
say hello, and this news makes me want to die. When I wake a
few hours later it is dark outside and the house is quiet. Still, the
manuscript is where I left it: fanned out across the floor, glaring
up at me.

I thought, I hoped by reading it I might find out that all along
I've been imagining things, that it's just in my head, that all this
worry, all this craziness, all this avoiding was really over nothing.
That I might feel silly afterward and call Father Mark to apologize and things would go back to normal, back to the way they
were at first, that first day when everything was good and happy
and okay and I was thrilled about winning the contest.

But I didn't expect this. Definitely not *this*.

His story . . . it's about . . . well . . .

I was just going to skim through it quickly.

Then I read the epigraph. A quotation from Thomas Merton.

I simply have no business being [in] love and playing around with a girl, however innocently . . . After all I am supposed to be a monk with a vow of chastity and though I have kept my vow—I wonder if I can keep it indefinitely and still play this gorgeous game!

And I remembered the poem Father Mark gave me, the love poem "For M. in October," and what Jamie said about Thomas Merton, that he was a famous writer, a famous priest, who fell in love with a young girl, his nurse, and they had an affair.

Then I began to read and once I began I couldn't stop.

He needed me to read this. That's what he'd said. Now I know why.

Father Mark thinks he is Thomas Merton and that I am his M.

"This Gorgeous Game" is the story of Father Mark and me, told from the very moment he and I meet in the school office at Sacred Heart. All of it is there, every second we spend together, every thought that goes through his mind. There is only one twist to it, a single, horrible twist that twists me and my stomach into agonizing knots.

In Father Mark's story we fall in love. He with me and I with him.

We fall in love and have an affair.

Just like Thomas Merton and M. We learn about love together, the meaning of love—his words. A gift from God we call it. *He* calls it.

He loves me.

Oh, God. Why me?

It is right there on the pages in gut-wrenching detail. He set a trap and stupid, naive me, I walked right into it and now I'm caught. Like an animal.

> *God must have extraordinary plans for such a creation*
> *as this.*

Father Mark writes this line in Chapter One.

I remember. I remember him saying this very thing to me.

And now I know. *I know.*

Father Mark has not given me a story, he's given me a proposition.

All this time, all these weeks, the meetings, the phone calls, the texts, the visits, the letters—so many letters and now, finally, I know.

And then I think how everyone loves him. Everyone thinks he's the greatest, nicest, kindest man. So did I. I did, too. I let him do this to me. I encouraged him. I practically begged him to. I wanted all of it, in the beginning. How could I have been so stupid? How could I let this go on for so long? Get so out of hand?

I crawl into bed, curling myself into a warm cocoon. When I fall asleep, I dream about Father Mark. Even in my sleep I can't get away.

It is a nightmare.

Father Mark is looking for me, following me, and I know he is there and he is approaching quickly. I want to run away but I cannot move. I am a sitting duck, a seventeen-year-old sitting duck of a girl, waiting, waiting for him to find me, corner me, trap me like a hunter's prey. He comes closer and closer and I can hear him breathing, waiting, drawing out this moment. He knows that I know he is there and he is pleased. He knows that I want to run but can't. He is enjoying this, knowing that he has me where he wants me. He likes this very much. Somehow I know this, in the dream.

I am afraid. Filled with fear. Paralyzed by it. Made of it.

And just when he is about to see me, in that awful moment when I am trapped by this endless game of hide-and-seek, *his game*, me hiding, me always hiding, him seeking without ever tiring of the game, the game I provide him . . . I am his game . . .

That's when I wake up. Right then.

I am drenched. The sheets are drenched, my pillowcase is drenched. I am shaking so hard the bed shakes with me. My blanket is twisted, thrown off to the side. I am uncovered and shivering. I can't stop the shivering no matter how many blankets I tuck around me. I am sick with nausea. That's when I run to the bathroom because I am going to vomit. Again. But I don't. I heave and heave and nothing comes out. I can't rid myself of him.

I stay in the bathroom, rolled up in a ball on the tiny green mat. I don't sleep because I can't be sure he won't come back and find me in my dreams. So I lie awake instead, until the shaking stops and the breathing slows and I begin to relax. Little by little, the fear leaves, and eventually, *eventually* the fear turns to hate.

Just like that, the fear turns to hate. Hate and anger.

And I am alone.

I wish that life would come to a stop. That everything. Would. Just. *Stop.*

Please, God. Make it stop. *Please.*

And then in one of the darkest moments, the thought goes through my mind that if he had stolen my wallet I could have gone to the police and said, *That man stole my wallet*, or if he had gotten in an accident while drunk and driving the police would have hauled him in and said, *You were drunk driving and with a minor and that will land you in jail*, or if he had just hit me, if he had just punched me in the face even once I could have gone to someone and said, *That man assaulted me*, and gotten him in trouble. These thoughts grow worse and worse and worse until the very last one, the worst one of all comes, *That it would be easier if he had just raped me.* If he raped me then I could go to the police and cry,

RAPIST! THAT MAN RAPED ME!

There would be physical evidence and they would take him away no matter how famous or beloved he is. They would lock him up and then he could no longer

Write me.
Call me.
Text me.
Follow me.
Show up at the house.
Leave notes everywhere I turn.
Invite me places.
Invite my family places.
Make me have to lie.
Write about me.

Teach me.

Love me.

God. Make. It. All. Go. Away.

Make *him* go away.

I want to erase him from my life. I wish I had a Father Mark eraser that I could wipe across his existence. And then Father Mark would become Father Mark and then Father Mark and then Father Mark until finally, after a while, he was just

Father Mark.

Until he was no longer there at all.

With this thought comes a single shred of strength.

Erasing Father Mark. I can do that. I have a way to do that. I see the irony of it, how this time around, I get to play the role of God.

Right then, I know what I need to do. For me. For *me.*

But before I move, before I get up off the bathroom floor and head across my room to the couch, I have one last thing to say to God:

Thank you, God, for this gift that is my writing. Thank you, God, for this space where I have all the power. Sorry though, God, because I think I'm about to fuck you over. Sorry ahead of time, okay?

Then I become God the only place I can. On the page.

I pull out my laptop and begin to type. *Click, click, click* go my fingers as they fly across the keyboard. I do not stop, not when the sun rises at dawn or the morning turns to afternoon and then to evening. I stay like this all day, writing, and everyone, my Mom, Greenie, my friends, Jamie, and Father Mark—of course

Father Mark—tries to reach me. They worry. They think some-thing is wrong. *Am I sick?* they want to know. *Will I go to a doctor?* they want to know. But I can't answer. Not my cell, not texts, not e-mails, not voices or voice mails. Not yet.

I cannot stop until I've made him go away. Until I've made this story *mine*.

Mine. Not *his*.

I am no longer God when I finish. I am neither God nor priest. I am once again just a girl. A seventeen-year-old girl. Olivia Peters. Just a girl.

Like. Any. Other.

When I finally close my laptop, I know I am ready. I call Jamie and then I call Ash and then I call Jada and I tell them, I tell them that I need them right away, that I need them to come over, and that afterward, together, we need to see Sister June.

ON MY SIDE

TAP, TAP, TAP GO MY FINGERS.

My right knee bobs up and down.

They can't get here soon enough. I might burst.

My mother is downstairs, sitting on the couch, worried, wanting to know why I won't talk to her. Tell her what's wrong. I am afraid she'll be disappointed in me, that I will find out her faith in priests is stronger than her faith in me, and I cannot bear that possibility so I decide to wait and see, wait and see what someone else thinks. What Jamie and Jada and Ash think. What Sister June thinks.

I don't hear my bedroom door when it opens.

A hand touches my back and I almost jump out of my skin but my skin stays firmly stuck to my body.

It's just Jamie. Just Jamie. *Jamie.*

"Olivia? Everyone is worried." He sits down on the couch, his hand still on my back. I am twisted away from him, facing the window. I fight the urge to shake him off. But Jamie will not hurt me. Jamie would never hurt me.

"Where are Jada and Ash?" I ask, so quiet.

"They're on their way."

"I'm scared," I say after a long while and turn, looking into his worried eyes.

"I told you: you can tell me anything. I promise. What is going on?" he begs.

"It's bad. It's really bad. You are going to be upset. Everyone is going to be upset."

"Olivia. *Please.*"

I force myself to look into Jamie's eyes and all I see is kindness. Trust. My heart beats so fast, so hard, that I wonder if Jamie can hear it.

Jada and Ash enter my bedroom and close the door behind them. They rush over, move the coffee table out of the way so they have room to sit on the floor.

"Livvy, we've been so worried," Ash says.

I am surrounded. Jamie to my left, on the couch. Jada at my feet, on the floor. Ash next to Jada, to my right, between the couch and the window, blocking my view of the space I've come to hate. For the first time in weeks I am not scared by my situation. I am relieved. Safe.

A long time passes with nothing said. My eyes bore out into space when I finally get up the nerve.

"I think there's something wrong with Father Mark," I say, and steal a glance at Jamie, trying to gauge his initial reaction. He doesn't flinch. I gather my courage. I look at Jamie one more time. Then I look at Jada and Ash. Their faces say, *Tell us.* So I do it. I finally do it.

I tell.

And Father Mark has made this part easy now.

The story he's written is gathered into a neat pile, again sitting on the coffee table with the title page on top. I lean forward off the couch between Jada and Jamie, tap the stack with my hand, and say one word only because there is only one word necessary to say it all:

"Read."

Because it's all right there.

"Why don't you go first," Jada says to Jamie. He nods okay, and she gives him the manuscript, picks it up off the coffee table and gives it to someone who is not me.

But I have more. I have plenty for everyone. Plenty to go around.

So I lean in a different direction this time, toward the place where Ash sits. I point at the Father Mark pile on the floor between the couch and the window, startling Ash who realizes she is covering part of it with her body, and again I say the one, the only word necessary:

"Read."

Because it's all right there.

And as Jamie and Ash and Jada read, when their eyes become wide with shock, that's when I begin to cry for the second time in front of someone else. Now I am crying because soon I will no longer be alone in this. I don't want to be alone another minute and I won't be. I rest my head on my knees. I am exhausted. So exhausted. Like someone sucked the life out of me. And I am nervous. So nervous about what I am doing. About telling.

About making this accusation.

I am accusing a priest. I am making accusations about Father Mark, a beloved priest, a beloved Father, a beloved author, a beloved professor. Someone everybody loves. Everyone.

Everyone but me.

When I hear Jamie put down the manuscript, causing Ash and Jada to pause in their ripping open, reading, and putting aside, ripping open, reading, and putting aside, making a new pile, I bury my head further into my knees, afraid to look at him, so I don't. I don't look.

"I've read enough," Jamie says.

"I think I have, too," Ash says, and I hear Jada sigh.

"So . . . what do you . . ." My voice fades.

"He's obsessed with you," Jamie states. There is no question. Only certainty. Jamie is certain for me.

"Extremely," Jada says.

"I know." My voice is tiny. I look up at them finally, my arms hugging my knees tight.

Their next question is written across their eyes. They don't need to say a word.

"I never, ever, ever, *ever* want to see him or hear from him or hear his voice or touch anything he's touched ever, ever, *ever* again. I don't want him to call me, text me, e-mail me, write me letters, leave me presents, write me stories. God, I want him to go away forever. And I want him to die." My voice is hoarse and low and I am startled by my own words. "But I messed up, right? I mean, because I never told him to stop. I never did." A lump fills my throat and tears slide down my cheeks. "I mean, look at all this." I gesture toward the letters and torn envelopes and what remains of the stack between the couch and the window. "I don't even know what they say. I haven't opened anything in weeks. I can't bear to touch them," I sob.

"You did nothing wrong, Olivia," Jamie says in a quiet voice.

"He's a priest. He's your professor. He's a powerful, public man. It doesn't matter that you haven't told him to stop. He never should have put you in this position, he never should have done this to you in the first place."

I take my hands away from my face and look at Jamie through blurry eyes.

"Olivia, I may be your boyfriend but honestly—and please keep my love of the Catholic Church, the priesthood, in mind here—something is very, *very* wrong. Something is very wrong with this man and it has nothing to do with you. You are not to blame. It's happened before, Olivia, to so many other people, and it is still happening to people and now it has happened to you, too. I'm so sorry, Olivia. I am so sorry that it had to happen to you, too."

I blink through more tears. I feel Jada's fingers weave gently through mine.

"Let's gather everything he's given you," Ash says, and stands up. Takes charge. "The letters, the invitations, the e-mails, whatever you have. And Sister June, I know you trust her—Jada and I trust her—let's call her now and tell her she needs to come over. I bet she knows how to handle this sort of . . . situation. You are not going to go through this alone. There are so many people who love you, Livvy, and who are going to help make this stop."

"Okay." My voice is a whisper. "Okay."

"Do you have her number?"

I gesture toward my cell, sitting on the table. This time I have no voice left.

Ash picks it up and scrolls through the address book.

For the first time since Jamie arrived however long ago, he touches my arm. And I am not alone anymore. Jamie and Ash and Jada are helping me. They take on my burden. They do it for me because I cannot do it any longer by myself.

ON HATING GOD

LETTERS. EVERYWHERE. PILES OF THEM.

Jada handles these.

E-mails. Most unopened.

Jamie takes this task.

Voice mails. Filling up my mailbox. And texts. Endless texts.

Ash has it covered.

They go through everything, all of it, systematically now, as we wait for Sister June to arrive. There are so many things. Almost too much to count. But count everything they do, because Jamie says it's important to know how many of each. How many in how much time.

My mother paces outside, worried. We'll tell her when Sister June gets here. We'll all talk together.

"What if she doesn't believe me," I whisper at one point.

"Everyone will believe you, Olivia." Jamie's voice is firm. Full of conviction.

"Because of the story?"

"Because of the story, yes. But because of everything else,

too. There's just so much evidence." He sounds almost over-whelmed.

Evidence.

"I hate God sometimes."

"Sometimes I hate God, too," Jamie says. "I think I hate God right now."

"But I hate Father Mark even more." Low sounds from my mouth.

Ash reaches up from where she sits on the floor and grasps my hand. "Try to sleep for a little while. Go to sleep. We're not going anywhere. I'll wake you when Sister June gets here."

Before I close my eyes I say one last important thing. "Guys . . . thank you. I don't know what I would have done . . . I don't know . . ."

"It's going to be okay, Olivia." These are the last words I hear before sleep comes and carries me away.

ON GOD'S ARMS

I WAKE TO THE SOUND OF VOICES.

Jamie and Ash and Jada and Mom and Sister June.

The story of me and Father Mark is told for the first time out loud, and it is Jamie who tells it for me. I listen and watch as Sister June's face and my mother's face go from concerned to shocked to outraged as they peer at the letters and other things. Then Sister June glances through the story, *his* version. "This Gorgeous Game."

"That's not even all of it," Jamie says to her—and before the talk of phone calls and lawyers and therapists and meeting with deans and bishops, before all of that happens, and it does happen— Sister June's arms reach out and pull me in. And next, my mother pulls me close and kisses my hair.

"Oh, Olivia." She is crying.

"He is stalking her," Sister June says.

Stalking. Father Mark has been stalking me. That's the first time the word is used and I'm not the one who uses it. Sister June does, then Mom, then Jamie, then Ash, then Jada, one by one by one, like dominoes falling down.

Stalking. Stalking. Stalking. Olivia is being *stalked.* I have a stalker. A priest stalker. A famous novelist stalker. I have a priest, famous novelist, professor stalker.

And then Greenie comes.

When I hear the story told for the second time out loud, *my* story, told by my family and friends, it is a different story. It becomes a story about a girl who is stalked by a priest. Taken advantage of by a priest. I learn that it's not her fault. How of course she'd be afraid to say anything, how it's scary to make that kind of accusation about someone like Father Mark, especially someone like him. How manipulative he's been. How I've been manipulated, how they've all been manipulated. Father Mark found shocking, clever, creative ways of getting to me, playing with me like it was all one great challenging game and me, his favorite plaything.

I am Father Mark's favorite plaything.

But not anymore. Because now, now I am surrounded by people who love me, and not that other kind of surrounded I've felt for so long—the threatening kind—and I am grateful after so long to finally feel protected. To not be alone.

My mother sits on one side of me on my bed and Jamie on the other, holding my hand, and Greenie on the floor nearby and Sister June on the couch with Ash and Jada. They sit there for I don't know how long. As long as it takes. As long as I need them to. As I go in and out of sleep, I think about everyone's arms around me, embracing me, loving me, and I think about the framed poem that is perched on a little stand on my mother's dresser. The one I've always thought so cheesy, that famous poem about footprints in the sand, the one where the narrator thinks those places on the beach with only one set of footprints are the moments when God has left her, even though God promised never to leave, and finds out instead that those were the moments when she could no longer walk, that the one set of footprints is God's. That God has carried her when she cannot walk herself.

I've never been able to give myself over completely, in that *I surrender to you, God* sort of way people talk about, that Mom and Greenie talk about as if it's something they do every day. I've thought before how this must be what taking a leap of faith really is. Faith is letting yourself fall and believing, *knowing* that someone, something, this being we call God is waiting there to catch us in a big, soft, God-sized baseball mitt.

I've never had that kind of faith before.

But I have faith in the people that surround me now, and I know, I *know* beyond a shadow of a doubt that they will catch me if I let myself fall. I *know*. And so I do. I let myself fall.

When I wake, everyone is still here. All of them.

And I know. I know I know I *know* that everything is going to be okay.

I no longer have to carry this burden alone.

I am not alone.

*It is not a game. That was
a wicked thing for me to say . . . If
anyone ought to know it, I ought.*

—THOMAS MERTON

ON GRATITUDE, REVISITED

IT'S A BEAUTIFUL AUGUST EVENING, ONE OF THE MOST perfect nights so far this summer. The dresses in my closet, untouched for so long, beckon, in particular the long white linen one with the blue sash. Slipping it over my head, I let the fabric fall around my body and look in the mirror. The reflection shows a girl I no longer recognize, eyes sunken from lost sleep, long thin arms, face gaunt from not eating enough. Hair stretched high into a tight ponytail.

"Olivia?" Mom calls from the living room. "Everyone is here."

This news sparks a smile—just a small one—but with it comes a glimmer of the person I've always known looking back from the mirror. I tug on the band holding back my hair and watch it fall around my face, a bit tangled and knotted, but I don't reach for a brush.

Better, I tell my reflection. It's just a matter of time when things will get better and better, and then maybe someday, all better.

I descend the stairs one by one, my hand gripping the banister, my feet a bit unsteady, until I reach the bottom and look up. This will be my first time out since everything . . . it all . . .

Began.

"Hey, Livvy." Ash meets my eyes with a smile. "Don't you look fantastic."

Happiness ripples across everyone's faces. Mom, Ashley, Jada, Greenie, Luke.

I try to copy their expression but can't quite manage to. Everyone keeps their distance. Or maybe they give me space. *Will things always be this awkward? Will I always feel this weird? Damaged? Ashamed?* For a second the urge to turn around and walk back upstairs is almost overwhelming. But it passes. And I stay where I am, both feet firmly on the floor.

Before anyone can say more, Mom ushers Ash, Jada, and me out the door and soon the three of us are walking along Commonwealth Avenue—Ash and Jada acting like my official chaperones for the evening. Jada has one of my hands, dragging me along—I guess I'm not untouchable after all—and Ash keeps us laughing with her nonstop chatter.

You can always count on Ash.

Before long we reach the tall iron gates of the Public Garden. The park is teeming with people enjoying the break in the August heat. Parents pushing strollers. Couples walking hand in hand. The sky is vivid with reds and pinks as the sun sets.

At first I hesitate, nervous to be out, to be so exposed, to be in a place where *he* could find me. Us. Or even just watch. See. But I know my family, friends, and Jamie are right, that I have to start somewhere, start taking back my life, and here is as good a place as any. Maybe even the best place because I care about it so much that if I lose it my heart might break.

Soon the bench comes into view, *my* bench, the calm lake, the weeping willow, and I see Jamie, waiting there like he said he would. Ash and Jada hang back, giving us some space. Then, when they are sure that I am okay, when I tell them it's okay, they turn to go, leaving Jamie and me alone.

"Olivia," he says when I come around to the front. He stands. "You look . . ." He stops, as if my appearance is not the best place to start. "I'm glad you're here. I was worried that maybe . . ."

"I'd decide this was a bad idea?"

"I guess. Yes."

"Well, I'm here," I say, sitting down. Jamie offers his hand and after a second's pause I take it and our fingers weave together, his warm skin surging with life like a shot of energy I've needed. "Back in our place," I add, and he smiles.

Then Jamie, his voice soft, like he's afraid it might sting, says, "There are movers boxing up Father Mark's office, Olivia. His nameplate is gone, too."

"Really?" My voice is hushed. I lean my head on Jamie's shoulder. I don't ask where Father Mark might be moving to. I don't want to know.

"Yes," he says. Then, "What are you going to do with *your* story?"

I'd e-mailed "This Gorgeous Game"—my version, *my* story— to Jamie after I told him about it, when he asked to read it. "I'm not sure yet," I say, and Jamie puts his arm around me.

"Don't worry. You'll figure it out. In time, you'll know what is right."

"Yes," I say, because it's true. I will. "I wish this was all over with. It's not, though. There is so much ahead to deal with."

"But the worst is behind us," Jamie says.

"Us?" I watch as he nods his head.

"Yes, *us*. Keep repeating that to yourself if you have to," Jamie says gently.

"Oh." I am unable to keep back the tears that spring to my eyes.

The sky turns from twilight to deep blue and the stars begin to brighten the night and we sit in silence, Jamie and I, on the bench by the lake under the weeping willow in the Public Garden. I think about "This Gorgeous Game," how it sits, stacked in a pile, on my coffee table. I think about how maybe, maybe someday, someone will publish this story. *My* side of the story.

"This Gorgeous Game" by Olivia Peters.

I can wait for that day. Even if it's a long way off. There will come a time when I can share this. When I *will* share it. But now, right now is for letting go. Making peace. Finding some peace.

Finally.

And that's the moment when I look at Jamie, really look at him, as if for the first time, as if I can see right through those big, beautiful eyes into the depths of his soul, his gorgeous soul, and I know this is not a dream, this "us."

That he won't leave or disappear.

He is real. This is real. And this relationship, this love, I know I want. There is no doubt.

I. Just. Know.

Eventually, after a long time gazing into each other's eyes, we rise and begin making our way back down the path toward the gates. And I am so grateful. I am so grateful as he walks me home, holding my hand, because that is all I need right now.

That is all.

ACKNOWLEDGMENTS

This story has been a long, intense journey, in which I have too many friends, teachers, and loved ones to thank for accompanying me along the way. You know who you are. My gratitude to those who read drafts—Lisa Graff, Lauren Myracle, and Marie Rutkoski. To everyone at FSG, especially you, Frances, for your faith and patience with this challenging project. To my agent, Miriam, as always. Two others I must name: Molly Millwood for your insight, and Michele Burrell for the same. And to Dr./Father/Monsignor Stephen Happel, who I know is still out there, somewhere, looking out for me.